T3-BUU-824

in memory of my father (1902-1961)

ACKNOWLEDGMENTS

Grateful acknowledgment is made to the following publications for permission to reprint copyright material which first appeared in somewhat different form.

Appeal to Reason
Backbone
The Berkeley Barb
The Berkeley Poetry Review
Berkeley Poets Workshop and Press
Berkeley Works
Beyond Baroque
City Country Miners Anthology
City Miner Magazine
Draconian Measures
Minotaur
ONTHEBUS
Open City
Plexus
Poetry, S.F.
The Realist
Room
Vagabond Press
Velvet Wings
The Wormwood Review

I wish to thank Mark Weiman, my publisher at Regent Press, as well as editors Claire Burch, JoAnne Scott and Penny Skillman whose assistance with the manuscript was invaluable.

FOREWORD

Someone once wrote — "only the dead tell the truth, and then not for some years." So too, the journal, the record of the past, tells the truth if you let it soak long enough. Over time, the flesh falls from the bones, and we get to the marrow of things. Our myths marinate and the symbols come to the surface. What happened is only history: what matters is mythos.

Most journal writing appears elliptical — thoughts skip like stones across the surface of a life. Like a seascape seen from a moving train, the beauty is glimpsed, rather than known. The trivial and the profound get equal time. The sincerity of the moment dies quickly in a journal; the first rush or gush of feeling loses its suds. Honesty comes only with a slow synthesis.

The pieces collected here have been synthesized from originals which were often too diffuse, too muddy for publication. But as Gertrude Stein said, "mud settles," and I have tried to take mud and make adobe bricks — enough bricks to build a small house for a kind of female over-soul.

Synthesis, like style, has something to do with sedimentation; the settling of the sand of thought and the leaves of emotion into a compost heap of prose from which a poem may grow. Or a story ferment. For some of us, the compost heap itself is worth study: *Even blue mold is a map of dream.*

In the conventional novel there is exposition and narrative leading to insight or what we used to call the ah-hah! moment. In school, we spoke of this as the vines (narrative) and the grapes (ah-hah!). I just wanted to crush the grapes and make wine.

Writing, as I experience it, means wringing out the heart/mind until it stops lying. In a journal, it is possible to gnaw on the existential bone all day and then use that bone to make stone soup for supper. Poems begin in the journal; and often abort there. Trauma reflected upon in tranquility can produce morally stunning insights — literary light! It can also produce maudlin rubbish. When I first began to rework the raw material in my journals, it was all I could do to separate the garbage from the trash. But I always return to the style of the notebook because the other forms bore me. "The way to recognize a dead word is that it exudes boredom," wrote Anais Nin in *The Novel of the Future.*

Gertrude Stein (America's quintessential language poet) wrote: "If you are a thinker, you will change the language. You will not use words the way others do." The way others do is still pretty much the same today. Prose is prosaic and poetry is exclusionary.

In recent years, there has been some hope that women might change the language. Virginia Woolf wrote that all the older forms had become hardened by the time the woman writer took up the pen, but the novel might still be soft in her hands. Woolf suggested that she might knock it into new shapes and use it as an outlet for the poetry in her — for it is the poetry, wrote Virginia, which is still denied an outlet. She wrote of the tyranny of the literary establishment: ". . . if a writer were a free man and not a slave, if he could base his work upon his own feeling and not upon convention, there would be no plot, no comedy, no tragedy, no love interest or catastrophe in the accepted style, and perhaps not a single button sewn on as the Bond Street tailors would have it."

Women, too, are slaves and not free *men*. Woolf wrote in 1928: "I thought of all the women's novels that lie scattered, like small pock-marked apples in an orchard, about the secondhand book shops of London. It was the flaw in the centre that had rotted them. She (the woman writer) had altered her values in deference to the opinion of others."

Expanding on this theory, which is set forth in her essay, *A Room of One's Own*, Woolf wrote that women are forbidden to write about the life of the body. They were/are inhibited by patriarchal taboo. Today, when bright-eyed young women tell me that this is no longer the case, I show them my files — the ones labeled "blood taboo" — together with the terse responses from editors who bothered to read my works on female biological experience. Publication is out of the question. When it comes to a woman's physical life, only the transmuted and abstracted material ever sees print. Oh, of course, Fuck Poems are in great demand. It's the maternal material that is anathema to the malestream editor. (I just edited *that* sentence into oblivion.) Writing about babies or gynecology or even about real female sexual needs is about as popular with editors and publishers as writing about skin disease.

Content is censored just as much today as in centuries past. Form is also severely censored and writers who go outside the lines when they draw pictures of the world are seldom rewarded for their efforts. This is curious because nearly every other 20th Century art form has cut loose from the past. Today, painting is about paint. Music is about sound. But words still cling to something very old. Like religiosity, language has its seat in the old brain, in the reptilian brain stem of early man. Chants are as old as the dance. In the beginning was the word, and the word was sacred. Sacred text became story and *we are our stories.*

We will never be without our stories — the fables and tales, legends and myths that surround us and comfort us with symbols and songs. As Joseph Campbell tells us, ritual is enacted myth, and our rites change as the myths do. Witness the rock concert — an ancient rite made new.

What modern writers need to find is the structure that supports words today. New age stories may not need ends, or beginnings, or even middles. Gertrude Stein wrote: "Stories have gone, just as representative painting has gone. Perhaps representative painting has gone because we have photography. Perhaps stories have gone because social structure as we have conceived it is going."

Many of the stories of Western civilization have been internalized in our culture. The post-literate generation can watch a ten minute video about the end of the world by ice or fire and no one needs to refer them to *Revelation* (although it might be nice). The young do not need to be told about original sin or the legend of The Fall. They've heard it all somewhere; these myths stain the culture.

It's my own hope that we're a bit sick of the old mythos, that we're overdue for a paradigm shift away from Judgement Day (dread and damnation as social control) and toward a new-pagan pragmatism — a genuine nature religion and Green Party politics.

If this is the direction of the next millennium, literature will get a break. We'll be able to let go of linear time, the sense of time that leads to death. Poets know these lines are only circles after all. And no matter where we go in time, we always meet ourselves coming back.

So, too, in the present work, I find the person who wrote these pages is no longer with me. But she meets me coming back through the existential steps toward consciousness. She is still asking questions. The answers are forgotten now.

Many of the individual pieces included have been published over the years in different magazines under the working title: *Loose Leaves From the Little Black Book.* I hope that placing them all together between two covers will make a kind of marriage. Reading over them now, they seem to have the aura of an old photo album in which what is left out speaks loudest.

Anais Nin once wrote: "Trust the fragments." With my own students over the years, the phrase I used was "trust the dust." Dust is never deliberate. Like the past, it just accumulates and becomes the ever expanding present. In the journal I can savor the moment and then *let it go.* Eternity happens when we can awaken into the present moment, the moment which includes all that has been. Then the moving finger's piety and wit move on.

Jennifer Stone
Berkeley
fall 1989

TELEGRAPH
AVENUE
THEN

"We watched the ghostly dancers spin
To sound of horn and violin,
Like black leaves wheeling in the wind."
        Oscar Wilde
        The Harlot's House

autumn 1966
Lafayette, California

Last year's Christmas tree lights are still strung out on the mantelpiece. One by one they burn out. It's August. September. There are still three lights burning.

early December 1966

I get a divorce. I'd rather be lonely alone. My next door neighbor buys my house. She wants to fix it up, she says, and rent it for income, she says. The driveway is buried in leaves. The trees and vines have grown over the long wooden porches and across the roof until the window grew dark in my bedroom. So now I will cut my way out of my *cul de sac*. I will leave the woods which are my back yard. The graves of dead pets will be deserted. The neighbor comes with buckets of white paint. One color she says, white or beige she says, then use accessories for accents. White paint across the

wooden beams of the ceilings, over the bricks of the fireplace, there is no stopping her. By the window in my bedroom there is a vine creeping up the wall. Once the roses
grew into the room, falling through the window. She paints
over the vine in her haste, then stops to scrape it loose and
cut it down. As I trek back and forth packing the trunk of my
car, I hear her muttering to herself, "You'd think nobody'd
lived here."

December 1966

Buy Indian tea, lemon shampoo, cinnamon candles and
a bottle of Irish Mist. Go to a coffeehouse in Berkeley and
pick up a man. Bring him home to desecrate my marriage
bed. Afterwards we shower. He looks clinically at my stomach scar and small breasts. I forget about the rites of passage,
the desecration ritual I planned. I reach out for affection,
bury my face in his shoulder and ask forgiveness. I guess we
have not seen the same movies. I expect the same response I
got ten years ago. He is about my age but he is still a young
man. Strange. I dress and light the cinnamon candles. I
throw pillows on the floor and logs on the fire and pour the
Irish Mist. Music and incense of course. Dutiful domestic.
My son falls out of his crib soaking wet and dreaming of
spiders again. I give him half a tablet of Valium and stuff him
back in bed before he can make a scene. I shut the bedroom
door tight. Returning to the fireside, I discover the man has
been impressed with me after all. He's drinking my liquor

and looking around. He grins, "You're ready for more, aren't you?"

January 1967

Wipe the peanut butter off the table and clear a space for myself. Ache with guilt. Take both sons to the childcare center and wait while Simon sits outside the gate, "to get ready," he says. He has to get his face under control. I am angry with him every morning now. Sure, I made him dependent. Sure, I let him think he could always stay at home with me. Hell, he's only four. At the first place I left him they had chickenpox and he got it and he has scars. From chickenpox. His older brother Sam has been to school before and knows the ropes. But suppose Simon is a sissy. Jesus Christ.

Then one day after school Sam tells me about the room at the center. The room with no windows where they put you in and lock the door and you stay there alone until you're all good again. An old lady put my four-year-old kid in that room every day. Shit, says Sam, my great big six-year-old kindergartner, everyone tortures little kids.

I get drunk. This is how it starts then, the self-pity and the whine of woman alone, woman with child on her back, woman with woe and wringing of hands and getting to be such a bore no one listens to her anymore.

February 1967

Simon is four years old. He doesn't say much. The ants were marching six abreast across the kitchen sink this morning. Simon made an ant house out of his plastic leggo blocks. He put a cookie in the house and went out to play. When he came in to replace the cookie with some cornflakes, he saw I had washed the sink with lysol.

"Mother," he said, "if you had told them you were going to kill them, they would have moved."

This evening he brings me two paper clips and asks to use the silver polish. I ask him why and he says the paper clips are ice skates for his mouse. I give him the silver polish and he goes to his room. No one needs to tell Simon he doesn't have a mouse.

spring 1967

Move to Berkeley. Give way to joy. Seven lovers now. I take the telephone to bed with me each night to talk to this one while that one sleeps beside me. I win for a change. How's this for power. Here's looking at you, kid. I ran into a brick wall and came out the other side. Now I wish to record the myth-shattering events of the afternoon of my life. Gangway, Edna St. Vincent Millay. Bunny [Edmund] Wilson said she had nineteen love affairs and just couldn't help it, poor thing. If I'm doing it, who can say I'm not the type. If only my energy doesn't give out. If only I don't get my scripts mixed. If only I don't get my throat cut.

summer 1967

We talk all night and he is melted gold in bed. I'd give anything to keep him because he allows me to be me; I may even say he encourages it, which is risky. He also has what seems to be an informed sense of humor and we laugh so much I seem to be getting healthy again. But damn it, sooner or later he drinks to stupor and one night he sat on the edge of my bed and set his hair on fire with his cigarette. I watched my family die of booze and fall apart like that and it terrifies me so I threw him out. But now, sometimes remembering, I wish I'd kept him anyway and buried him in the back yard when he died and poured libations of bourbon on his grave.

September 1967

I bought this honest-to-God topless bra at the most esoteric lingerie shop in Berkeley. The European woman who owns the shop looks down her nose at the locals, taking no solace from girls who go braless. "Come back and see us when you need a good brassiere, my dear," she smiles, rolling her r's.

When I try on the topless bra she assures me it is the last one in stock this season. I buy it because it gives my breasts a terrific hoist. I look in the mirror and imagine I am the Empress Josephine with my breasts shoved up under my chin. Black lace-covered sharp bones lift and frame my flesh. The first time I wear it, I get black and blue marks. Poor Josephine. Napoleon said, one time or another, that women have no rank. Their place in life, their socio-economic score, depends upon the males with whom they find favor. One can find a good master, or a wise master, or a louse, but it's still a slave system, any way you call it. A rich master may be kind and generous but you have to stay home and pour drinks for his friends. You have to. Well, the women's movement is seeping into my psycho-sexual adjustment. What can I do with an unused topless bra? I am what I throw away.

autumn 1967

I read my old college diary. Where were you in '52? In the wooded womb of a west coast women's college, I was staring at the rain. Long nights the eucalyptus trees beat at my window until a windowpane broke and the rain blew across my room. I was from Southern California and this was *ultima thule* for me — the ultimate limit. It was a scene from *Wuthering Heights*: the storm beating at the heart, the pathetic fallacy that nature sympathizes with human moods, echoes the ache of souls in torment, whatever. It was because I was eighteen and in love.

I was in love with a jaded Jewish student of the high-strung, bitter sort. I talked to my old teacher, one of the Cassandra sort and she said, well my dear, you must study the romantics. Romantics tend to act out their passions as well as to write about them. It's tradition. You will find that a stoic life style is wiser, but it takes time. Some of the English Romantics were stoic, she said, but it made them sick. You, she told me, are a hell-bent romantic and you may burn out and never grow old enough to become more than a cynic. Romantics die young or get killed fighting in Greece. Once they mostly died of tuberculosis, but since antibiotics there is only neurosis and cigarettes to substitute for T.B.

Well, she said, you'll find out. If you need one, there is always a revolution going on somewhere — always a front for liberation, even at home. Some few are chosen, but I don't think you're the type. You've got a low pain threshold, haven't you? Well, perhaps you'll come through it all. If you get through love and the theatre before you're thirty, you may amount to something. Always remember, classicism is health and romanticism is disease.

She said lots of things like that: comedy ends in marriage, tragedy ends in death — that sort of thing. She advised me to keep a diary or journal, to record the events in the moment. She said that if I did that, when I was her age I could look back and see what hit me. I looked up diary in the dictionary. It means: "lasting one day." One day at a time then. One page after another adds up to a life.

My diary from that time, the early '50s, is filled with events: plays, dance, books consumed, clothes bought and worn out, people known and worn thin, an endless stream of feelings pouring out about who I was or wasn't. I am sorry to say that I burned those pages a few years later. I was afraid someone might see how much I cared about all the men everywhere saying how it should be, how I should be. Men, the real romantics. The ones who made me up, who trapped me in their imaginations. Poets, lovers, writers, fathers, brothers, teachers. I was mired in their mythos. Of course I wanted their approval, their love. The Lords of Creation, Charlotte Bronte called them.

Whatever they are, they sure as hell seem to have things under control at the moment. And they had me under control as a girl. Even when I was rebelling, it was always their movie I was in. I burned the journals because it was too painful to remember the kind of fool I'd been. Something on the order of *Tess of D'Urberville*. Thomas Hardy's tragic Tess who fled from vile seducers and has to hide in a *cul de sac* in the woods with dying birds clustered in the trees above her.

Tess was my model! Hiding in the woods surrounded with wounded birds shot by the hunters during the day. All night while she slept in the leaves, the victims of the "sportsmen" bled on her and fell dead while she tried to sleep in the dark. At last she kills her seducer to reclaim her honour (what Hardy imagines her honour to be) and the long arm of the law catches up with her at Stonehenge — why did she flee back to the sacred place, the pre-Christian site of ancient rites? It was the right instinct but the wrong era. After they hang her, the virtuous man in the story gets her younger sister as a consolation prize. I think it was her younger sister. Anyway, someone pretty.

Well, I've been to Stonehenge now, and there's no refuge there. I'm done with being a sacrifice in the land of the patriarchs, and I've forgotten how to be a muse. I'm done with love for love's sake. It takes too many week nights. In the diaries I have kept, I have played all too many parts. Now it's time to file my report. I've done my living. I've done my lying. Now I can edit the agony. A dozen pages will keep.

fall 1967

> *"Writing a journal means that*
> *facing your ocean you are afraid*
> *to swim across it, so you attempt*
> *to drink it drop by drop."*
>
> George Sand

I run into my love in the rain and we are not lovers yet. I tell him to kiss me, it is my birthday. It's not, but I never tell the truth about trivia. We *have* seen the same movies and gone to different schools together, so the nostalgia can begin even before the pain.

fall 1967

I sit before his fireplace, reading my poetry.

> In the grass some small blue bones
> Distinct fragments of vacant lots
> Perfume behind the fossil where I lie
> Forgotten as my father's tennis balls . . .

"Never mind your bizarre productions," he yells, "talk sense or get out!" Pours himself a drink. Then he begins to laugh. He has tattoos of black cats caught in spider webs on both his arms. He blames that on his mother. "Free association, hell," he mutters. "You want stream-of-consciousness, I'll give you stream-of-consciousness." I will censor most of what he said because this is my book and I want to. I give only a few lines:

"Faggots use a lot of laxatives and that's no shit. Paranoia is belief in the Devil who was not your Daddy Man, no matter how much you wished to be his spawn . . . Pandora's box is a lonely erogenous zone, my own, my own sweet Martha Lorraine. Sealed in vain, sealed in vain, Pandora's box is sealed in vain, it's perfectly plain. Panic is not the fear of fire, it's the fear of passion, the fear of the great god Pan running around rutting the world to the ground. I tell you this so you'll shut up about your soul, girl. I'll tell you where your soul is, you're sitting on it. You're in heat and you write some gibberish and think I'll listen to it. You'll be sorry when I'm dead and gone, you black-hearted bitch."

Everyone agreed he acted badly at the end.

October 1967

What was it he said to me last night; "Beloved Pussy," he said, "you've got the baby and I've got the ball." He goes in for the D. H. Lawrence stuff, the blood coming out of the earth bit, the ships that clash in the night theory of sexual encounter. He doesn't mix up lust with love the way I do. It's the same old yang-yin mess. Like when I want to get in touch with my primal self, I sit near the entrance to a cave on the beach. I wait for the sea to give up her dead. I wait for the tide to turn and then I read the seaweed like tea leaves in a cup. He, on the other hand, wants to make it with a dolphin.

October 1967
(symposium: in ancient Greece, a drinking together with music and singing)

This one is different. My children are gone for the week. We are alone and in love. We scrub each other's backs and feed each other strawberries and lie on the floor and drink wine. Gratified desire, satiety, the works. We walk out to a cafe-bar to pity the loveless world. We are so knowing and so self-satisfied, everyone is drawn to us. We are holy and they want to touch us. We don't speak often, only to confirm each other. The shared laugh of seeing through everyone we meet; *Tout comprendre c'est tout pardonner* . . . we forgive everyone. And when we are alone again the gong sounds like it does in the beginning of a J. Arthur Rank film and we are drowned in each other and if it weren't real it would make a swell movie. It's never been anything like this except once when I took acid, but the man I was with then was far away. This time he's more me than I am and we have been here together many lifetimes before and we are drinking each other alive. This is the moment to die. Nothing can get better. Nothing does.

Halloween 1967
(frigidity made simple)

For crissake doctor, he had his damn *bonsai* tree in the bathtub when I got there and he told me to hold a paper bag for the trimmings. When he finished filling up the bag, he sent me out to the garbage to dump the twigs and stuff and he told me to be sure and bring back the bag. I had to fold it and put it in the kitchen cupboard.

That night in bed with him I dreamt he was standing behind me in the line-up at the bank as I was trying to write out my life (anyway, I think it was my life) on wooden ice cream spoons or popsicle sticks and he pushed me out of line before I could cash them in . . .

At breakfast I asked him why we never went anywhere together any more, and he said who the hell did I think I was all the time, Joan Crawford for God's sake and I said I thought I was Sappho at Stonehenge and he said, who needs it.

November 1967

Love, like alcoholism, comes to a point of no return. A brain gently simmering in booze will go soft and the fragile cells will shudder and die, burning out like matches. It's not the heart that breaks, it's the nerves, the spirit that sinks. It's the nerves which become infected with the disease of love, with the knowledge of another and the corruption of deceit. Thought breaks the heart.

I indulge myself, writing notes in a drunken delirium of maudlin self-pity. "You always told me I enjoyed my suffering. Well, someone should. Men bring out the masochist in me." Later I find these notes scattered on my desk, in my purse, pinned to the walls and scribbled across the kitchen cupboards. Thus begins many a female's literary career.

But the material is all derivative. I write in roles: Medea, Lilith, Desdemona, Ophelia, and Camille writing in lipstick on my mirror. I want my own version of the burnt child reflex. I want to give a form to my suffering. I want to call the police. Leave town. Of course, it's all melodrama. I'm exaggerating. I cannot make the grapes weep wine. Who said love is our failure to understand nature? I'll live through this. My epitaph: She was there but she didn't care.

(the same November night, later and louder)

Put on more records. *Eartha Kitt purrs, "Hey Jacque, have you seen Louis? Is he still in Paree. I've tried. I can't forget. I love*

him yet. Hey Jacque, tell Louis, for me." It's the witching
hour, here sits the witch. Which witch I wonder. The old
Irish one; the Raven of Babble. *"Jezebel heard of it; and she
painted her face, and tired her head, and looked out at a window."* Christ was a virgin. Kept his nose clean. Didn't fool
around.

Ration the wine. Just another cup. *"Goodnight Mrs. Calabash, wherever you are."* The wine is spilt but the calabash is
not broken. The people upstairs are banging on the floor. I
yell at them: Mau Mau maidens from the African sand, how
dare you say that to my mask? A stranger in a strange land
belongs. If you think about it. Sensible D. H. Lawrence
ladies live in their loins. Lonesome loins are a liability.
Dorothy Parker said so; she also had monthly cramps and
hangovers and if I stop drinking then tomorrow morning I
will begin a bestseller: *Frigidity Made Simple.* There's sure to
be a hell of a market soon. Pass out for crissake. *"Goodbye,
Mrs. Pappadopoulos, and thanks."*

black next morning coffee:

Romantic love, like poetry, is a kind of homesickness;
the kind which made medieval monks sleep in their coffins.

end of the broadcast day

watch little white dot disappear
into infinity
remember the incredible shrinking man
remember his last words hardly heard
somewhere, in some dimension, I still exist

when I hear the voices they are speaking
I hear them meaning me and saying they —
aspirin, hemlock
clocks and graves
if I buy an electric shaver I will not cut my legs
if I write letters, refusals will come in the mail
if I go on a diet, the rest of the world will starve

there is a night wind there in the trees
    I have hung windchimes among all the branches
    that is how I know

autumn 1968

> *"I know thy works*
> *That thou hast a name,*
> *That thou livest and art dead."*
>
> Revelation 3:1

With my darkest eye I see my village today. Artaud's red ivy in the autumn covers houses near the park. When I see lovers lie beneath these leaves, I think of mongrels mounted in the dark. My thoughtful friends sit on the grass, all hugs and humor. I see a pack of monkeys grooming salty scales; they chatter and grimace, scratching one another's patchy scalps and crotches.

At the end of my village street I come to an open place in the rock; the ledge is precarious and covered with moss. There is a cave-in, or a breakdown here. I know this is the window, the end of the labyrinth, from this place I can see the end of this world. I'm in the limelight at the back of the moon. The mirror breaks, the sea covers me. Seaweed meshes are tangled around my throat.

I haven't answered the telephone for days. I'd have left him sooner if I'd known.

autumn 1968

A black Republican in a stuffed shirt. Calls Martin Luther King a slaughter ram. Male supremacist, always lords it over me. Paternalism at best. Phallocentric. Never lets me off without the full treatment. It's getting to be a lot like work. Sexual slavery. Interesting. He pays back, but always a little less than he gets. Always takes his turn first just in case I lose my temper which I have been known to do on some few occasions, at which times he cuts out and leaves me alone to stew in my own juice, as it were. He has never wasted his evening, not for years now. Never lost his control over me. To punish him I must punish myself — not see him.

Last night we went to a party with some Hebrew professorials. It was low-key but pretentious in its own way. He tightened up as we entered the room and I watched him turn on the charm and make everyone laugh. I considered that maybe he had to do that to stay alive. I said as much to him when we were alone. He agreed in his way and said pickaninnies were smarter than greys and used their wits. I told him I thought it sucked. The world sucks, he told me. Not me, I said. Rather than be a slave, I'll be buried in my grave and he said yes, I probably would. He said I should learn to dissemble and attach myself to a male with power enough to protect. I said I didn't date silverbacks.

It isn't that I didn't really love him, because I did. It isn't that we weren't really happy, because we were. But we couldn't exist in the world. We were alone together as if we'd both been married to someone else. We came together like a pair of adulterous sneaks. I know about the pecking order. I know about the sucking order. I know why there's so much sad in sadist. What I still don't know is, in all this, why me.

Halloween, 1968
(the same shirt)

Why me, I asked him. Why not, he said. Little kids come to the front door and scream when they see the real skull in the window and me dressed like Snow White's stepmother. He's coming over after my kids go to bed. He called me to tell me so. He asked who was I going to be this Halloween, The Grey Lady? Well, I told him, I hardly know what to say to an Afro-archaeologist like yourself. You've got a sense of history all right. You just come on down digging away at these ruins, dragging my alabaster ass out of the archives and down your street. You come on up here to call my home a catacomb, rip off my shroud, break my stone tablets and tell me my life is a lie. You call me an anachronism, you seething paranoid dumb buck; do you really think you know who I am . . .

I hang up, turn up the Kabuki music and put the ancient skull by the bed. I light the candles. The White Witch rides again. Wait till he sees the bats.

midnight

He calls back. Innocence, he says, is of the spirit. Naivete is of the mind. He gives me his diagnosis: you cannot stand what you understand. You must have been a Catholic in a former life. He hangs up, adding he'll come over when I snap out of it.

winter 1968

I met a man in a radical therapy group. He gave the impression of warmth and civilization. I wasted the usual hours making myself attractive before seeing him again. I wanted to be sensual and civilized. The first time we were alone together he read me Charles Bukowski's story about a Venetian mermaid: *"The Copulating Mermaid of Venice, California."* It's about two drunks who steal a cadaver, discover it to be the body of a beautiful blonde woman. They rape her remains and swim her out to sea. This was the first stage of his foreplay. I dropped a cup of tea in his lap to make sure he could still feel. Then I read him the autopsy of Marilyn Monroe. It left him cold.

summer 1969
(how to waste precious time with the wrong people)

We take my children to the lake. When I lie down under
a tree he starts playing with my bathing suit. I get up and tie
myself together, walking off on the path that circles the lake.
The children hit the water and get as far away from us as
they can. When I return to the beach, he says walking off
like that means I intend to reject him. I suggest I need the
exercise. He assures me he's more than meets the eye (we
met at a nude party). Yes, I'll probably have to reject him.
They seldom leave you any choice. He goes on to tell me
that he understands vaginal orgasms aren't the whole truth.
A man's best tool is his hand. He lists his qualifications: he's
had a vasectomy, his wife has left him, etc. I send the
children for ice cream as soon as they surface. I ask him to
reserve sex talk for private places. He tells me I'm a prude. I
agree as energetically as I can. He tells me he's free because
he's been through primal therapy. It's hard for him to relate
to me, he says, because I've never even been "in group." His
wife refused primal because she thought the best thing for
her self-image was to keep it. That's why he got divorced.

I confide in him. I explain to him that having children is
a primal experience. It was primal enough for me and it's
probably primal enough for anyone living in the late twentieth century. My first delivery was induced with some intra-
venous stuff. It was like an auto accident. The second time I
had to pull the baby out with my own hands. Damn doctor
said he was premature and might go back in. I made stone
age noises and everyone in the delivery room was thor-

oughly disgusted. I fill in this story with lots of detail. My
companion hastily joins the children at the ice cream bar.
Primal slime is fine but I wouldn't advise it on a day-to-day
basis. (I know where I came from and I know where I'm
going, but I'd rather let that alone.)

My beach companion has returned and settled down to
eat himself into oblivion. Now that I've finished with the
subject of primal, I decide to tell him what I think of groups.
There's the academic group. Great folks. So open-minded
and generous. There's the pervert group. Every morning I
walk to the subway and see males from six to sixty standing
under little bridges, urinating into the creek, waving their
penises at me. Grand group. And then there are friends.
What about them. Take some of my feminist friends, the
ones who are strictly party line. My old friend Sonia said to
me the other day that I must be careful what I said on a radio
show I planned to do. She said, of course, I was clever but I
said some dumb things too and she was afraid I'd shame the
cause. My basic trouble, she told me, was I thought I was a
novel. Then she came to my apartment and said my sons
were male chauvinist piglets, regular studlets and all. My
Apollo! My Dionysus! Of course I wasn't man enough to tell
her to stuff it. Women don't respect you unless you domi-
nate them. So much for friends. So much for groups. Remember school? Remember those groups on the playground?
Once I did go to an encounter group. Curiosity and peer
pressure. It was back in the days when I still used expressions
like peer pressure. It was a weekend marathon and it cost
forty dollars. In one exercise we were supposed to remain
silent and feed each other. A young male kept trying to stuff

some foul-smelling cheese down my throat. He was one of the facilitators. I kept shaking my head and spitting the stuff out. He blew his cool and told me I was anti-anal because I couldn't stand the smell. Damn right! I said. Also stupid as hell because I paid cash for this therapy crap.

It is for these and other reasons I live alone now. I should say I live with my children, but my generation describes women without permanent mates as women alone. As I finish my lecture and observe my male companion, it's a comforting thought. I do live in a group and we are very lively. Sam is an Aries and Simon is a Leo. Three fire signs under one roof. I'm a sad Sagittarian with nothing left to lose now, except of course, this little black book I'm writing.

summer of People's Park, 1969

I live near the corner of Grove and Oregon in West Berkeley. There is plenty of trouble on this block. My next door neighbors have barbed wire around their yard. I've gotten used to police cars and chaotic noises. Even so, last night was alarming until I realized I had left the radio on and it was only John Cage.

This weekend I'm taking a course in African Literature at U.C. All about the tragic elite in Nigeria. I've been reading for weeks and I know all about these Nigerians who write in English; their sense of loss and their nostalgia for a past that hasn't even passed. Most of last night I read Elichi Amadi's novel *The Concubine*, which is all about a woman who belongs to the sea. The Sea-King sees to it that it is death to marry her. Yes.

In the morning, Saturday, I am still in the dream, in the place where symbols are the things themselves. Walking out the front door I hear helicopters circling the town. I see a jeep full of Asian males in military uniforms. I come back inside and turn on KPFA public radio. The newscaster is playing *The Internationale*. Then she says something about the maintenance of order on the campus. I can't see very well because I read so late but I go out on the porch again to look at the soldiers. They've won, I thought; they're Vietnamese and they've won and it's peace and everything's settled.

I stand there drinking my coffee and looking at the men in the jeep. They're speaking English. Like the African writers I'm reading, they speak in English. Does that mean *we* won? Finally I talk to them and ask and they are Koreans and they are in the American army and I can go to class they tell me. Things on campus are settling down.

Simon sees them and he wants to show them his American bomber plane. It hangs from the ceiling in his room. He earned it one day at the Induction Center in Oakland. All the demonstrators were so sincere, and liberal ladies like Joan Baez and her mother went to jail and the best people were there. Sam and Simon were dressed as Vietnamese peasants. They were in a play on the street; the bomber came and killed them. It was made of papier-mache and Simon asked if he could keep it and the man who made it said yes.

fall 1969

Another Berkeley afternoon on Telegraph Avenue. You can be just as lonely here at the Grand Hotel. We sit in the cafe. Ms. Magdalene, in her tie-dyed hair shirt, sits with the young males. "Take me for a ride on your motorcycle." Eva Braun rides again. Suttee Sal claims a mate. They all wind up dead: bumped off in a bunker, sent to a guillotine, hanging headless next to Benito, all loyal to the end. You can't tell them anything, is what I say. They nibble rolls and digest cigarettes, talking to Byronic boys with greasy hair and perfect teeth.

Sing of the sad cafe: the suburban dropouts: Zorba the sneak; Lord Jim, the narcissistic darky who admits he sold his own brother to Barnacle Bill the Sailor, as Bill barges in with a size Hemingway fish slung over his shoulder, sealed in a plastic bag.

In the street our leader is playing frisbee with the police. These are the days of the flowers. On a clear day you can see San Pablo. They gave Timothy Leary a tangerine and some scraps . . . some scraps . . . some sea weeds, some dry kelp . . .

This is the sort of scene which surfaces when cannons fire to raise the dead. They say the noise of guns brings up the drowned ones who hide at the bottom of the sea. They leave the darkness of the deep and we remember . . . we see the floating debris . . . it is the debris, you see, that distinguishes us . . . one from the other . . . that muck on the surface . . .

What debris did you see? . . . flowers floating in the hair of corpses, the fairest cheek, the whitest hand . . . rots in heaps on the sand . . .

"Better dead than dying," said the veteran at the bar who came back to tell us we fucked his war . . . leaves swimming with the raw sewage on the crest of these waves while the surfer clings to drifting wood and the mermen slip below . . . old condoms drift to shore near broken bottles in the sand castles near the sea moss at the foot of the cliff where the caves draw back and whisper . . .

Winter 1970

> *"And unto them was given power,*
> *As scorpions of the earth have power."*
> Revelation 9:3

When the neighborhood rapist appeared in my bedroom at three o'clock one morning, I was sure it had happened before. I recognized the feeling as if it were death. I knew all along it was coming. *Deja vu.* Black, with a hat on. As gently as an ancient, I asked him what was the matter. He told me. I comforted him with all my skills. He assured me he wouldn't hurt my children if I did what he told me. He had been through the house and seen the boys' blonde heads on their pillows. What he could see of my room in the dark made him think I was Asian. I could have been. I could have been anything. Geisha woman or goddess.

What must be understood is that he believed me.

A man found a ladder in the basement and broke into my home through a bathroom window. He threatened the lives of my children and would not let me move or turn on a light. And under these circumstances I convinced him he'd made me happy. He promised not to frighten the children. He was lavish with his compliments. He said I had a snatch like a sixteen-year-old. All his misery poured forth. He talked about the lousy treatment he'd gotten from women. All they needed was a rod in the right place, he said, then they knew who they were. I consoled him.

He began to give me advice. He told me how careless it was to come home late at night. A carload of friends had driven me to my door about midnight. I'd forgotten my key and gone around to the back, making a lot of noise and calling attention to myself. The porch light was on, he said, so he could see I was wearing a miniskirt. He told me he could break into any house in the neighborhood and what was I doing alone in a place like this, was I on Welfare? I told him I was a high school English teacher and he was very impressed. He told me I must learn to be careful because this whole neighborhood was full of real bad men and they could be watching my house.

Finally he got out of the bed and said goodbye with a sort of wistful sneer. He would go out the back way so as not to wake the children. After I heard the door close I tried to get up. I moved to the end of the bed. Some time later I heard a dog howling somewhere. I tried to get up again. I walked along the wall until I came to the back door. I locked it. I got to the living room and lay down on the sofa. After awhile I could hear the birds outside. I found the children buried in

their sleeping bags and I unzipped the bags to make sure they
had enough air.

It's been a long time now. I sleep in my clothes. I lock my
children in their rooms and lock myself in mine. Sometimes
I sleep on the sofa next to the phone. The worst thing is, I
don't know what he looks like. Black and high cheekbones
but that's about all. Every time I see a black man with his
profile I have to wonder.

Finally I move. Retrench in a safe neighborhood. It's my
own fault. I thought I was a white man. I thought I could live
as I liked and the world would love me for being myself. Zen
slap. My encounter with the facts. I've got to forget it. It
happens all the time.

The nightmare always comes back. It's always the same
and it's always different. Sometimes he comes through the
walls; sometimes he just drops by with friends and I suddenly
know it's him and he was there all the time without my
seeing and when I realize this I can't breathe and I am
smothered awake. It's the feeling of suffocation from fear, it's
the *I can't scream* dream.

When the police took me to the hospital I was afraid to
give my name because my older sister works in the medical
records office there and if she found out what had happened
I'd never live it down.

1970
(nightmare three weeks after the rape)

A tornado crossing the plains is her fallopian tube sucking up the earth and all its creatures into the maelstrom,
chewing them gently as it sinks and spreads out into a
vagina, collapses into hundreds and hundreds of little vagi-
nas, all hairy and sweaty and rowdy and punching each
other and shrieking and running off into the mountains and
leaving their nightgowns thrown on the sand.

She is the only one left now, alone behind a barrel
cactus, clinging to the thorns, hiding behind the yellow
desert flowers, staring in terror at a mottled gila monster*
climbing up the other side of the cactus, his heavy tail
sluggishly following him and his hideous tongue lashing
from side to side. His eyes do not see. She hisses and spits at
him. When the gila monster reaches the hairy hysterical
little vagina with her pink nightie on, she jerks and panics
into a rabbit held by the ears.

The gila monster's tail erects and swells as he snaps his
jaws shut, locked into the little bunny's belly. The monster
vomits all the rotten, undigested, lethal muck from his tail
through his heart. The poison puts out the sun.

Now the cactus and the sand are burning in the darkness. They are scalded and blistered as radiation begins to
rise. There are seashell skeletons rising to the surface of the
sea. Hollow bone fragments orbit the earth. Earth herself is
honeycombed and porous now. Everything falls away, crumbling like a cracker.

*Gila Monster: A large stout lizard with a rough tuberculated skin and thick tail, found in the arid regions of Arizona, New Mexico, etc. It is pinkish, or dull orange and black in color and of sluggish but ugly disposition. It sometimes obtains a length of about two feet. Also, a closely allied form, H. horridum of Mexico, which has an entirely black head. The bite of these lizards is venomous. Called also beaded lizard. Its digestive system is primitive and most of the food ingested is left to rot in its tail.

Christmas, 1970
(around the bend)

There is life beyond politics. Once upon a time we looked for it beyond the pale. Then it was called the Kingdom of Heaven. Now it is found beyond belief and now it is called a psychosis.

spring 1971

This morning I went to see my acupuncture man. He's an ex-shrink. You're getting away with murder, he said. Now I know why he's an ex-shrink.

Of course he could mean the cosmic murder, the silent acquiescence to evil, the daily death of spirit, the gentlemen's agreement to ignore it; or perhaps he meant the collective conspiracy, the illusion that we die one at a time. Or maybe he was only being personal, mentioning my melancholy and advising me to wear bright colors. Black is back.

I like my mourning and I designed my death wish to go with my dress. Mine are the ruminations of an atrophied soul. It's true my higher self wants me dead, but the bitch won't kill me. If I died, I'd miss me quite a while. I watch the man slip a needle into my Achilles heel. Of all of us, I tell him, it's me I'd miss the most.

May 1971

Last night I talked too much again. I've got to stop talking so much. If I talk all the time like that, he'll think I'm so terribly lonely. That's what they think if you talk.

summer 1971

This bright sober morning it seems to me women are infinitely superior as a sex, but men are somehow better. I think that what I mean by that, or what I feel I mean when I say that, is that woman at her best can only express or personify that which is best in me. A man, on the other hand, is that mysterious other, my animus, my subconscious self, and is therefore the source of my dream.

My dream? My day-nightmare. Turn back the sands of time. Let's live it over again. Sit by the stone wall at the foot of the seacliff and listen to the wind in the cypress trees and the surf hitting the rocks. See the ashes of a beach fire blowing into the sunset. Hear my father calling me home. Cross the iceplant to the stairs that lead up the rocks to that beach house in La Jolla in the early 1940s. My mother is in the kitchen, pouring her first drink.

"Are you lonely," my father asks her.

"Not always," she answers, rattling her ice. They begin their ritual argument. (See the plays of Henrik Ibsen and Harold Pinter.) I run to my room to turn on the radio and drown out the sounds of my parents' pain. My sixteen-year-old cousin is sitting naked on my bed with a full erection and a lewd grin on his face.

I tried to sleep in a cave on the beach that night, but the Shore Patrol found me and brought me home.

fall 1971
(*sex and money*)

On the way home from work this evening, I walked down to the beach to watch the sun go down. I tried to count the men I have known, really known and liked or even loved, but didn't work for or sleep with.

There's my father, long dead. My brother, long dying. One childhood soul mate lost at puberty, and one more.

I can remember thirty-nine lovers and thirteen bosses.

winter solstice, 1971

I went out with this Tibetan vegetarian who hung his dirty shirts all over his living room, and he told me that, "Whatever is, is to be adored," but I didn't.

April 1972

The empty chair, the silent morning, the serene sheets; at last they comfort me. It all belongs to me now. I know there's more to understand, but I've come this far and this is enough.

Is wisdom more than love. What do men do when gods die. Grow up, I guess. Come out of their caves and pull themselves together. Life without illusion; they say it's good for you. Brave new world, without dependency; without the significant other, what Virginia Woolf calls the arm to lean on.

I must believe the thing will get better; the people will grow beautiful and wise. What in hell am I saying. Nothing changes.

Write about love and say what I know . . . what I know.

# # #

As It Was in the Beginning, Is Now
And Ever Shall Be

the furniture, the furniture of home
skins of wooly mammoths
faint flickering fire
the smoke and the stench numb the sense
stones, tools, and the paintings of the great beasts
    breathing from the walls
    and from the ceiling
steam from the pot boiling on the stones
sea creatures boiling in their shells
abalone bowls in the hands of children
all of us waiting for his shadow to return . . .

July 1972

Yesterday wasted. All the space taken up by my reactions
to Ann. Her father married my sister a few years ago. She has
discovered me, chosen me as her mentor, and fled her suburban existence for life in the fast lane. She's dropped out of
college and flopped down on my sofa to find herself. I'm
overcome by her thoughtlessness, my vision of my own
higher sensitivity, heightened awareness, transcended consciousness, la-de-dah. I'm high-strung. My nervous system is
frail; thin epidermal wall, raw ganglia wince and jerk with
any psychic vibration. The existence of others plagues me. I
resent them. With Ann, my energy is dissipated in irritation.

Why doesn't she pick up all her snarled hair out of the tub when she shampoos. And her dependence. Always asking: cigarettes, tampax, kleenex, toothbrush, toothpaste, phone calls, food and water for her dog, errands without end, fetch and do for her and on and on to anger and guilt for not telling her to take care of herself because even *that*, even telling her to shape up or ship out, is more effort than I want to make. I'm a coward when it comes to confrontation. Ann reads me letters from her mother and spins her wheels endlessly about why others are so unfair to her. I talk and talk and try to explain the world. I pontificate and waste hours saying how things should be. I use poetry and philosophy to impress her. I burn with wisdom. I challenge her not to neglect her (of course I'm talking about my own) royal romance with individuality and independence which would lift her (me) into pride and into the vanity of capacity and holding on and taking up her love in her arms and carrying it into the valley where she was born — finding the primal source and the vision sought always and found at last and known completely only to be left once more on the sand beside the forest sea as one life ends and the next begins . . .

(I found the above note about Ann. It was written two years before she jumped off a building, trying to kill herself. She can walk again but spends most of her time in institutions now. Why didn't I tell her what I really felt. Maybe it didn't matter. She wasn't much for reality, I see that now. But all that ephemeral junk; I might as well have told her virtue is its own reward. I'm not saying I could have helped, only I might have talked to her once instead of to myself.)

summer 1972

> *I started Early — Took my Dog*
> *And visited the Sea*
> *The Mermaids in the Basement*
> *Came out to look at me —*
> Emily Dickinson

To Mendocino with Greta and her dog. Greta and I have shared the same wine ever since we were sent to the Dean's office together for sharing the same man one night at a campus lawn party. On our way up the coast, we stop in the Pygmy Forest. Buds I hadn't expected so late. Involutional nostalgia for this place where I've never been. I missed it so. It is my childhood in Maine which I never had. A dream of a place I wanted to find, back then when I began to look. The old inn here is the place where I met my lover once and we were together in a way he will not, of course, remember.

The innkeeper says no dogs. Greta is furious at this injustice and I follow her to the beach while she rages. We watch the sunset. The outrage over the rejection of her dog is just a cover. She's really here to weep over a married man. I figure it's my job to listen, after all, she drove.

"He doesn't know me from Eve," she fumes, "and he's getting old. He's got hardening of the categories. He calls me his *mistress*. He thinks I'm the *deepest* broad he's ever met." She begins to giggle as we get to the bottom of the bottle of wine we bought at the inn. I lecture her on the limits of love: real love as a desire for the other person's good; neurotic love as a desire for the other person. Love hath an end, I pontificate, so work for the night is coming.

"A few phrases in some anthology won't keep the worms away! A few scraps of paper can't save you." Greta finishes the wine. "What if you don't work out, kid? What if you don't get in the Big Book?" She staggers a little as she gets up and calls the dog. He's mad with joy, running after the sandpipers at the edge of the surf. She pulls me off the log and we trudge towards the stairs that lead up the cliff. The ache is in the bones now, not in the blood. Wine hurts my head, not my heart.

"Life comes in clots," she sighs. "Your clots are just lots of words. Mine happen to be the last emotions of a lifetime: he's probably the last man, the only good thing I've had in years. Of course, he's killing me." We put her dog Regret in the car and go back to the inn.

In the morning we sit by the sea. We take tea. "So like the islands," I opine. "So like England and Japan. So concise, so refined, those two. Compact compressed cultures, with repressed peoples. No man is an island, but England is. A state of mind. Japan too, microcosms of their parent continents, chips off the old block, but more synthetic, tighter than mainland Europe or China. The people quintessential. Distilled . . .."

"Christ! are you going to be like this all day!?" Greta yells. She wants to be alone and not talk. I have the day to myself. I sit on the beach for hours and watch the sea palms that grow on the rocks. Rooted to shore rock, they claw their way into the stones. The surf beats their marrow souls. They bounce back like India rubber after each thunderous wave, all cartilage and gristle, grown from the depths of stone.

Greta joins me, after all, and watches the waves beat the kelp. Little phallus stems erected time after time, getting it up after each new wave. Then, finally, churning to death on the rocks, dying in brine at the tide's edge, bleeding iodine.

So too, Greta and her lover. Piercing the air with their sharp sea smells. Filling the seascape. And all the lovers before them, back into time. Back to primordial time when there was nothing breathing, no creature breathing in the deathy swamps, in the time when Earth was daughter to Sea.

And that was the time when Earth rose from the depths of the night and stepped onto the sand, holding in her hand the sea palm, the phallic sceptre; she knew the world as it was in the morning, in the beginning, and as it shall be once again after we have drowned.

Greta says if I'm going to go on like this, she's going to take Regret and drive back to Berkeley. She says she came here to *get away*. What's the good of all my writing, she wants to know, if it doesn't stop my grousing. I don't write, I tell her, I engrave.

Watching her drive down the coast with her dog's lugubrious face pressed against the back window of the retreating car, I consider that I have two solitary days for a final engraving. For this I need heavy metal tools. I'll have to fast.

The next morning I am not so much euphoric as just fey. I decide to swallow black coffee and kiwi fruit. Still, by late afternoon the absence of real food begins to have an effect. I find myself alone in the Pygmy Forest. It feels like the bottom of the sea. These whispering trees remember the waves, the surf echoes through the leaves. The air's so empty now, after the weight of the sea. Gravity groans in the wind as boughs ache to hold themselves above the earth. Everything's so heavy in the air. Land plants creak in the breeze. Forest ferns so frail — no guts. Lace-like brittle nettles crushed by a look. No resilience. No fluidity on land.

I feel beached like the sad dry things growing out of the earth. Thrust ashore from the red gardens of the sea; the tide went out without us. Left us to become stone and fossil, reaching toward a night light in the dark.

Once, mother was a dolphin, lit with marfire, the phosphorescence of the sea. Once there was an amniotic pool of bliss, and now there is a road and an inn and a dog named Regret. Consciousness creaks like the arthritic limbs of these twisted trees. If only the knowing would stop. If only I could stop.

Resting here. Seeing all that's past and all that isn't. And the next thing. The next humiliation. And will I be alone? Humiliation is better taken alone. Growing old is not a thing to watch. It cannot be forgiven in others. Alone, it can be borne. Even indulged. Alone, I can remember that I have not always been myself. I can see myself as another, and forgive her. I won't let her suffer any longer for what she did not do to them. Nor will I let them punish her for what she did not do, nor for what they did before she came. Finally, in the silence of the ages, so loud in this forest, it is possible for me not to hear what was not spoken.

Sea moss covers the blood stones here at my feet. Stones in piles like cairns at ancient crossroads. Drowning in the echoing air, I hear voices from the realm of faerie. I eat foxfire from the dying wood—the luminescence of enchantment—sitting in the center of the faerie ring. It's no use. They will not sing for me. Once the mermaids came in drugs and drink, but that was years ago and I could swim. A washout now. No sea in sight.

I must walk now. One foot after the other. This is Thursday. It's closing time in the West. The gates slam shut. The money's made and the vaults are sealed. We go no further than this Pacific coast. This is where we jump off. This is land's end. I say it aloud here in the forest where there are sacred Indian hearths in burnt-out tree stumps; charred glossy bat-black, bedded with pine needles and fern.

Crawling into a dead fire, a hearth pit in an ancient home, I warm myself in the ashes. The faces of my ancestors rise before me through the smoke. I look up into the sky, through the great cold waves, until I see flowing above me the pearl-green kelp beds. Life's light filters down through the dark blue indigo sea. At last I see the face in the glass-bottom boat and sink through Indian despair.

I wander out to the coastal highway and hitch a ride back to Berkeley, getting home after midnight. The next day the world sinks to its old level. Or I do. Greta comes over to say she's sorry she ran out on me but she can't stand my sadness. I'm pleased she takes me seriously and I show her my notebook.

"Oh Christ, Euphoria," she groans, "you're all wet. 'Too

much of water hast thou,' kiddo. Ophelia floating on a sea of
permanent waves." She thumbs through the notebook until
she finds a scrap she likes. We sell it to *The Berkeley Barb*.

SAND

VISTA POINT at MENDOCINO
is the
EXTREME WEST POINT
of California

read the sign there
by the sea

RAW SEWAGE
THIS BEACH
QUARANTINED

I've gone about as far as I can go amidst the garbage
and the flowers,
and SHE is standing on the shore in my long black cape,
costume in the wind
back to the sea with thee, love

There she was
and I saw her,

TYPHOID MARY
IN BEADS

September 1972

> *"Lilith chose to leave Adam and live alone by the Red Sea. She found peace there on the hard-rock-sand lining the deep blue gulf of Aqaba, making love with satyrs, minotaurs, and centaurs."*
> Hebrew legend

I'm reading about Lilith, Adam's first woman. There are so many interpretations I feel free to see it my way. Some say Lilith was Adam's first wife or mistress or companion and created equal with him, both of them made by God out of the dust of the earth or of red clay. It seems they had irreconcilable differences and she split with her demon children. Custody is destiny. Whatever. She left him to Eve who could melt into him and be part of him because Eve was made of his flesh. Or of blonde apples or something. So Lilith is the dark earth woman who lives alone at the edge of town like the village witch. Oh, I remember now, she *is* the village witch.

It was not Adam I loved all these autumns. I waited for her, for Lilith, to come home in the night and watch the storm with me. Together we waited for the winter foam to blow through the sea caves. The men I loved, I loved alone. That was in the spring, I think, when I needed the children. I remember how it was then. How I raved and wrung my hands and tried to *explain* myself and *he* said I was mad. So I was. And so I loved as I was told to love and he said how it should be and so it was, for him.

Then autumn came, and understanding. It was not man then who gave me life. I looked beyond the houses and the money and the sex life. The sex life. Lilith's children were born to me in the darkness. I knew my mother and kept silent.

All Hallow's Eve, 1972

The closer I get to forty, the more I study the dark ones. Lilith, the demon mother goddess, the dark lady, the literary cliche, the scapegoat, the death witch. Lilith is the dark night of woman places, the womb tomb out of which we came into the light.

Simon listens to my thoughts and sits singing, "A womb with a view, and you . . .." He should care. He's found an Eve. He sits on the grass with a grilled-cheese blonde who is all sunlight and smiles. There she is — his immortality. For her he piles up stones and pyramids and volumes of what he calls thought and blood and gold and gods by the dozen. All this so she'll create him anew.

Lilith, like Adam, is out on a limb. They're single. They are made of the same stuff, those two, and like Adam she's alone. Unnatural for a woman, men say. Thus: the strange one, the sorceress, the shrew, the bitch, the seductress, the pariah.

I bump into Lilith from time to time. Last time I saw her she came to a coffeehouse poetry reading. She rubbed cunt

cheese behind her ears and tied herself to a crucifix with
ropes of knotted sanitary napkins. She called it a feminist
protest. Her eyes were dark and heavy like those of Sappho.
Her heavy lids closed and she smiled as each poet threw a
stone until she fell.

winter 1972

> *"O dream with black wings,*
> *Mayest thou come when sleep*
> *brings forgetfulness . . ."*
> Sappho

It's an old dream: the sea lace caught around his throat,
the blackish fronds resembling cords across his chest as he
drowns silently in underwater slow motion, sinking below
the reef at the cove. I call it my Little Mermaid dream. I tell
people I saw a boy drown when I was ten. Actually I only saw
the dead body on the sand.

Dreaming, he comes to me in stillness and holds my legs
as if we were in water. I reach out for his hand the way I
almost did once before and then I hold him as I have always
wanted to hold him; in reconciliation without desire. There
is swimming in twilight on the crest of the wave and then
sitting quietly on the sand in the dark, watching the lights
go on in the town.

When he sees the lights, the dream cracks and becomes
verbal. He has an appointment in San Francisco. We say the

usual things in our old ritual. He decides not to use my phone. There is no point in asking him why. The rite of remembering ruins the dream. I wake up.

It's better to remember the good stuff. Once he touched a bracelet on the dresser, picking it up as if it were a lock of hair. Once he stepped on a kitten in the darkness of the hall, and he was angry, *really* angry with me for not remembering to put it back in the box. And the times he said he loved me with as much conviction as doubt.

I wish I could remember the end of the dream. Who is it said existentialists never finish their books? Being is too much with us. We can't finish until we know the end. Death is the end of knowing.

He's been gone a year now. He was not an existentialist. He was not even a swimmer. The last time I saw him, I stood on my front porch and shut the door behind me so the children wouldn't hear and I cried into his shoulder while he tried to sort of pat me. I remember I was quite upset and made such a scene he was caught off guard and he handled me as if I were a slightly sandy, wet puppy he didn't want in his lap.

December 1972

Reste En Hiroshima Avec Moi

He: You saw nothing in Hiroshima. Nothing.
She: Nothing. Just as in love this illusion
exists. This illusion of being able
never to forget. So I was under the
illusion that I would never forget
Hiroshima. Just as in love.

Hiroshima Mon Amour
text by Marguerite Duras
from the film by Alain Resnais
Grove Press, 1961

I am seated alone in a chair by the sea. The colors are
slate or navy grey and the sea is full of floating debris: broken
planes, shells of ships, Dunkirk desolation wreckage, all
drifting so quietly, rising and falling with the swell of the
waves like kelp on storm mornings.

This continues and stretches to the horizon. It is almost
dawn, but the darkness will remain.

Now *he* comes to get me there. I am wearing only my
navy trench coat over my skin as I used to do when we
played at clandestine liaison love before the war.

As I begin to unbutton my coat, the top button crumbles
and breaks off in my hand and when I try to pick it up, there

is nothing but seaweed on the sand and some little dead crabs by my bare feet. The road *is* sand here. There is another road of rock. Then one of dirt.

These roads lead from the beach up the cliffs. I take the one at the more acute angle away from the tire tracks.

A miniature broken S T A G is along the path to the Tokyo Honeymoon Hotel. The little stag is dying.

He looks at me and I see him. It is the child's feeling when the china doll breaks and even the pieces are kept in a box.

The little stag is made of a magic porcelain and seems engraved with an antique A S I A T I C pattern, which seems to be a language.

January 1973

I go for a drive with a new male. His name is Oscar. He's been passed on to me through an old friend so I can't be rude. I'm not anxious to begin a new liaison; I have enough to do as it is. My primal attachment is grim but steady. Secondary attachments have fallen into place. A New Yorker flies into town with paternal presents. A youthful beauty who imagines he's the picture of Dorian Gray comes back to me after his ritual debauches, saying he simply has *no respect* for any other woman. Each one is a poem. Oscar appears to be a zero but I decide to look him over.

We visit the dead in the hills of Oakland. My mother's best friend's last lover is buried here near a willow tree. His tombstone is engraved,

Fall leaves, and graceful be . . .
Farewell then, I follow thee.

I show the grave to Oscar and then tell him all about my mother's best friend and how she met her last lover on the pier at Aptos by the sea. Oscar is not listening. He murmurs that our mutual friend has told him a lot about me and what she has told him makes him feel we should get to know each other. He says he hopes we will fill each other's deepest needs and he just loves this graveyard. I tell Oscar, yes, the graveyard is very beautiful and I'm grateful to him for bringing me here to see it. Oscar tells me about his therapy program. Before therapy he was afraid of his own shadow; *apres* therapy, he doesn't even cast a shadow.

Oscar is very proud of what he calls The Appian Way — a road of very exclusive tombs done in mock Roman or pagan styles with pretentious statues and columns. Mausoleums stand with chained, rusted gates where the dead are locked in. At the end of this road is a toy pyramid as big as a house — a woman's last resting place. Did she buy this for herself. No, it is dedicated to a "Beloved Wife with Eternal Devotion." Her husband has laid her to rest in a mummy's tomb and there is no way of knowing if she asked for it. What would make a man do a thing like that, I ask Oscar. He tells me if a man truly loves a woman, there is nothing he will not do for her.

We walk to the older, overgrown section of the graveyard which is in deep shade. I feel as if I am walking through a Southern Gothic novel. Stone lambs mark the graves of children: Gertrude Kiekenveldt, aged 11, died 1881. Sarah, wife of Thomas, lies among five of her children, all gone to feed the roses. The stone slabs are engraved, "Lambs of Our Lord." Some of the graves are still visited. Shreds of wreaths and weathered urns rest on the stones. Libations and sacrifice, here and everywhere. The pagan and the Christian. Always there are stones; the souls are in the stones. Engravings on the older tombs of Sarah's children are formal: "William James the II," "William Paul," then "Our Jonathan," and "Little Polly," and finally just "Eddy, aged 11 months." Sarah, wife of. Did you make these redundant decaying fences 'round the graves? Did you watch beside a bedroom fireplace in a room with high ceilings and candles lit for prayers? Were you ashamed to sleep? All those children gone to gardens in the night. The leaves are deep and time is silent here. I could be quiet here and rest in this great stillness if only Oscar would stop talking data. Ratio of abortions to live births in the United States, etc.

"Oscar, did you know that Charlotte Bronte died of pregnancy?"

"Indeed no, she died of tuberculosis or phthisis, as it was called in those days."

"Yes, indeed, of course, but don't you see, the presence of the fetus, the parasite, brought about the consummation of consumption, what is called galloping consumption, and finished her off."

"Well, the thing is she didn't die of pregnancy but of T.B.," and Oscar goes on to say he's not interested in literature so much as he is interested in architecture. That is the reason why he brought me here to this graveyard, in order to show me the architecture and explain it to me.

Sarah has been dead for seventy years. In the stillness these graves at my feet are grey and alone. Ashes of flowers drift around these little cairns; wild grasses and tangled vines smother the mother's grave. Did she love them more because they died, these babies? Did she dream of the pill or use a vinegar sponge? Do I pity her or envy her?

Walking through these dark trees out of the valley of the shadow, we come to a hill with highrise graves. Stacked like moldy memos, the freshly forgotten dead lie in filing cabinets to the sky. Pulley ropes run up and down so flowers can be set before the drawers. Plastic roses twine about the handles.

I remark to Oscar that I intend to give my mortal luggage to a medical school. He tells me a thing like that would sicken my children and those who love me. Could be. And if I'm buried, could be someone will remember I'm molding away each year. That's what I remember when I think of my own dead. What's left of mother after thirty years. Perhaps the mass of bronze-gold hair that grows now on my tallest son. Perhaps not.

Oscar shows me an effigy of two lovers with their hands clasped about each other's necks. They are carved upon the door of a little cement cabin. Sex and death. Graves broken open through time; possession and violation. Let us mold together love. The rose grew 'round the briar. I tell Oscar

this is the old Heathcliff syndrome. Oscar says, yes, it was
Heathcliff who ordered the sides of the coffins to be broken open
so his (Heathcliff's, not Oscar's) dust might mingle with Cathy's.
Oscar goes on to say that men in general are more concerned
with what happens beyond death. They are the tomb builders.
They are even the artists for this reason. I tell Oscar women are
just as afraid of death, only they understand about babies and
making room. Then I get mad and remind Oscar it was Emily
Bronte, after all, who *was* Heathcliff, her creation of the demon
lover. She says so in the book; "I *am* Heathcliff." Of course she
was Cathy as well. For Oscar, my conversation has lost its
thread. He interprets Emily Bronte as a 19th century spinster
who loved her brother Branwell and was hung-up on her father
as well. To bring him up to date I tell him Emily was a pantheist,
although her passion for the universe (the moors, the earth, the
heath, the chthonic gods) had to be given a persona for the
purposes of writing a 19th century novel. I go on about Jung's
theory of the animus — the man within. Heathcliff as Emily's
other self. She wasn't writing about good and evil or about light
and dark. She was writing about the dual nature of the soul.
Schizophrenia, says Oscar; *dementia praecox* for sure, exacerbated
by sexual repression. Then suddenly, without warning, Oscar
goes into a tirade. Women, he yells, are always out to devour
men and get everything they can in this life and/or the next. His
own wife walked out on him and took everything worth having,
including his night light. After that no one needs to tell *him*
about women. I stop talking. Oscar's panic is fear of the great god
Pan. Oscar has a shadow that goes in and out with him. He is not
capable of caring.

We pass out of the graveyard, walking past the monuments of 19th century men of moment or megalomania. Terminal edifice complexes in marble, stone, and cement. One grave a block long ends in a fountain. One refined soul has chosen to be buried by a natural rock formation. The scene is bizarre, baroque and truly beautiful all at the same time. This place is as beautiful as any park or rose garden or seascape I know. No one's here today. We've walked for three hours. I haven't seen a living soul.

# # #

By six o'clock we are sitting in a Chinese restaurant. Oscar instructs me in the use of chopsticks.

"I've always done it this way," I tell him. "I can't remember where or how I learned. I just do it this way and it's faster. I'm hungry."

"That's wrong, that's not the way to hold your thumb." He tackles the noodles with his chopsticks and the waiter rushes to bring him a fork. I decide it's time to amputate. I go to the phone, come back to the table and tell Oscar my cat is very sick. We actually had a cat some years ago. His name was Arthur and his grave is in a suburban backyard. I tell Oscar that Arthur is barfing all over the rug and I have to go home at once. I tell him that if there is any throwing up at my house, it is catching and my children throw up too and I leave it to his imagination what a hell of a mess it can get to be. A friend is driving to pick me up, I tell him. I lie whenever I can. It gives me the illusion of power. Oscar is glad to get rid of me.

I slump into The Maenad, a woman's bar with a few women in it. I need a drink. A bubbling black female jumps up, gives me a big hug and assures me that I'm OK, and don't forget it. Damn dizzy dyke. I find some women who are not without conversation but we are interrupted by sneering young Bacchae in various stages of the inertia that passes for hostility in this community. I'm in for it. It's Gertrude Stein who first used the word "gay" to mean what it means, I tell someone. Isn't that sad, says someone. No, says someone else; what's sad is that Gertrude didn't say how it was between Alice B. Toklas and herself and let the shit hit the fan. I remind them what it meant to be a woman in the 19th century. I mean it was OK to be gay among friends but not in print. It was OK for Sarah to bury five children but not to undress for a gynecological exam. I talk about the trip to the graveyard and how Oscar loved to see the little temples where Greek maidens hold up the roof with their heads. Someone tells me any woman who still tries to relate to men, even in graveyards, is retarded in her psycho-sexual development. Could be.

Everyone is getting younger everywhere. I miss the androgynous Shakespearian scholar who used to sit here every night and rise above it all. She went back to New England. Perhaps people are older there. I try to listen to heterosexual women. They sound older; they weep to the old tunes. They're still in love with love, in love with Sam, all in love with Sam, the piano player in *Casablanca*. Terminal nostalgia. I talk to them about Anais Nin; a romantic woman's woman. She said Henry Miller couldn't love. He could fuck but he couldn't love. I talk about writer's impotence and Henry's hang-ups until a young Maenad goes bananas. It's obvious, I'm counter-productive. This is no place for me. I go to the bar and talk to the bartender; the wise and mellow black mother of us all, our Sibyl. Serene and beatific, she pours me a beer, tells me to be an honest cannibal and admit my compact with the devil. I ask her if *she* ever has any problems, if anything ever bothers her and gets her upset. She waters the ferns and sighs, "just women." Me too, I tell her, only in my case there's only one.

###

By ten o'clock I'm in a smoke-filled back room at The Blind Bird. An old beard, a candlemaker, holds forth on the subject of the male spark or fire which ignites the clay or the earth matter which is personified by woman. He says the life force is in sperm and it's this life spark which sets matter moving and gets the old earth off her ass, so to speak. I ask if this is the medieval theory of the homunculus or "little man" said to travel through the mother's body as if he were in an oven, emerging as if he were a clone, without taking any DNA from the female. The old beard says what the hell, he will buy me a beer.

"You probably think I'm a male chauvinist pig," he opines.

"Frankly my dear, I don't give a damn." I drink the beer. The jukebox plays Joan Baez singing *Love Is Just A Four Letter Word*. A joint passes around the table. Another beard leans toward me saying, well actually, the Women's Movement is very significant, very significant. Did not Marx say that social progress can be measured by the position of the female sex. First beard makes an obscene remark.

"But suppose I'm Ms. Marx and suppose I say I don't want social position. I want to be an artist." They tell me to be serious. The truth is, I answer, you men pay too high a price for your masculinity.

"As for me," I tell them, "I just want you to know that I did not attend the Hookers' Masquerade Ball in San Francisco last Halloween and I did *not* win the prize for The Costume in the Worst Taste, and furthermore, for your information, *I was not even invited* and it hasn't destroyed *my* confidence in myself as a woman."

The men grimace. Assuming I'm too drunk to talk sense, they ignore me. The women move in. Kirsten suggests I see a psychiatrist. Maria tells me to "give way to Joy." Monica suggests I be successful artistically, that I "be somebody, that'll show 'em." Karen sighs and says stay home and play the gramophone and cherish the hearth and worship the Buddha in all its forms.

I am half Irish, the worst half, and booze tends to make me rave. This is not a goddamn play, I yell. I am not a goddamn actor. This is my life here, now. Maybe I deserve to be a slave. Men put me on for years and I bought it. I used to fight for male approval, that pearl beyond price. But man is not an oyster. Man is very irritating but man is not an oyster.

No one is listening to me. I pour another beer. Once I joined Women's International Terrorist Conspiracy from Hell (WITCH). I called up my primary attachment, old

number one, and I told him I was through. He laughed and
told me to come over and help him clean up his swanky
apartment. Every morning a man dressed like a mortician
hoses off the cement in front of his building. I, on the other
hand, go out every morning with a broom and sweep the
broken glass off my front steps. No place that's safe will rent
to children. Old number one tells me again how much he
needs me to help him fix things up. I don't do windows I yell,
and I'm not gonna be your nigger no more. I'm gonna get
revenge. I'll go be someone else's nigger. He laughed and
approved of my sense of humor.

                              # # #

The bar is closing. I move my glass in circles, looking at
the ceiling with its gold lanterns; a cafe in a Van Gogh
painting. No one's talking to me now. The woman who used
to play guitar here, years ago in the fifties, begins to sing
Foggy Foggy Dew. My memory goes back to an old scene.
Early love across the table drinking mulled wine. Did I ever
really love without bitterness? Sure, there were no resent-
ments until I had children to worry about. Marriage wasn't
so bad. Of course his apartment was a mess when I arrived.
He told me he'd saved the mess for me, so I'd have something to do. Busy little bride, I was. I scoured and polished
my way to feminine perfection. With rubber gloves over my
manicure, I did the walls and ceilings with lysol and ammonia. I douched, dolled up, cooked, decorated and buffed
everything to a high gloss. Turned out in a few weeks there
was nothing left but a vacuum. Literally. My husband be-

came an indifferent lover once I was available all the time. Sin had worked for years. After a few months of legal liaison, he had to be reminded. It got to be too much trouble to get ready. Those were diaphragm days. I found a lover who made appointments. Once I was all dressed up I wanted some place to go. I guess I've gone. It's kind of a funny thing; a psychiatrist I once went to told me he believed that females were the "grudge carrying" partners in most relationships. Could be. Yes. Could make a new bumper sticker for women: "Don't carry a grudge, carry a gun like the rest of the boys."

spring 1973

I need new glasses. I have an Asian optometrist. Laconic Dr. Lee. Well, he opines, I'd advise you to get tri-focals dear lady. Bi-focals won't meet your needs. With your perspective, that is with your present prescription you can see very well at a great distance. With bi-focals you'll manage to see a good deal of what is under your nose. However, you must know there is a vast area in between which is forever misted over with doubt . . .

I wonder if it's true Asians conceive the eye to be a primary erogenous zone. It's the look that lasts?

1973

> *"What is poetry and if you know what poetry*
> *is what is prose."*
> Gertrude Stein

The second year of trying to be a poet in Berkeley. Poets give me their work: great loaves of prose made into lots of little lumps and a few crumbling cookies; a great tree of prose hacked into kindling with a two-headed axe and slung over to the left margin and sawdust everywhere. Some sense some times but no song and reading aloud the sound makes no sense but the poets all say yes that is what I meant you see.

At the workshop I talk about the integrity of the image cluster and the definition of rhyme as similar sounds at regular intervals and the poets throw things at me. At the readings I never know whether to write something or dye my hair mauve. Theatrics or thought? I'm learning. I'm going to be contemporary. If I want to belong, I'll have to write polemics in poster form. I can do it. Mother always said I could adjust to anything.

w h o r e s

wendy isn't living with peter pan any more (actually they couldn't get it on for a meaningful relationship because peter was too mean and wendy wouldn't work) then wendy joined the women's movement and read g e r m a i n e   g r e e r

and now wendy says we're all whores whores whores and that's
it, that's where it's *at*, all right, all right and destroy the monetary
system she says so we won't be whores any more

i knew damn well i could relate to that and hell yes i said
that sounds all right all right, all right and get thee to a
barricade and make some w a v e s

and i ran to tell a man i know and he smiled and with
paternal patience smiled again and then he asked was i a
good whore or a bad whore

and i hollered do you ask black folks was they good slaves or
bad but he couldn't relate to the question maybe because
he's from the colored generation

. . . . . Not only do I plan to destroy the integrity of the image
cluster in my work, I intend to go for the puzzle (as in
crossword) poem, and to use free association without reser-
vation.

even seagulls get seasick

wendy met this liberal fig leaf this granulated student with an edifice complex he told her all about the ah-hah experience Nietzsche nihilism and naked apes but he doesn't have a car

if we could speak what would we say

do you remember do you remember those babes in the wood i think one of them left the phone off the hook let us consider the telephone as a sex object let us not

where are the snows of y e s t e r y e a r right here dear

my druid blue b a b i e s unborn went back to the sea it was still there

Truly, Gertrude, it is very difficult to use words without making sense. In that sense you were truly a genius because you have said what wisdom does and you have never made sense of it.

1974

> *"Why don't they read the way I write."*
> Gertrude Stein

Gertrude Stein said the most important thing about the work (writing) is someone who will say yes to it. Alice said yes to Gertrude and so the writing continued. I need someone who says yes. A yes man. I try to say yes to myself but there are these doubts I thought you might help me with. Oh, not you, *him*. When I ask a him, he always has reservations. Doubts. Oh he may admit I have talent. You know. A talent of sorts. One man didn't think I had the discipline. Another didn't think I had the follow-through. He also didn't think I had the overview. The next one didn't think I'd ever get it all together. Some thought I should write the way I talk. Others thought I should write logically and use an outline so I'd get somewhere. Another one thought I should write honestly instead of facetiously, in contrast to the one before that who thought I should write satire and send it to the *New Yorker* because that's who I really was, really. This lover thought I should write about the agonies of love because of my passionate nature and that lover thought I should write about frigidity and a third about lost love, about not being loved, about him actually. A woman told me to write about my children, about childbirth, abortions (I was ashamed to tell her I'd never had an abortion), the woman thing (or question), woman as victim, woman as goddess, whatever. I'll tell you what. I'll write about me. Whoever that may be. I'll call me the Piltdown Woman.* A real fake.

Damn, how do I shut out their voices? No way. Well then, use the anger. Write about how much I get sick of voices telling me who I am. That's what I'm doing, isn't it?

Piltdown Man: an elaborate anthropological fraud which was discovered when errors were found in the relationship of the fragments, some of which were from real human skulls . . .

winter 1974
(doubts don't go away)

What are these editors after? I study their letters and when they say a thing is wrong they use words to describe female sexuality: fragmented, loose, repetitious, abstract, diffuse, tangential, muted, free associative, subjective, circular, dreamlike, intangible. When they say a thing is right, they reveal their phallocentric focus. They want me to follow the main thrust, stick to the point, tighten it up, strengthen the climax, simplify the action, and keep the lights on, *literally*. It's embarrassing but it's anguish when I understand what's happening. It's not their fault of course. Virginia Woolf says it's no use going to the male writers for help, no matter how much one goes to them for pleasure.

Simon says I'll never make it. He says I'm always in a dither. I tell him his existence blocks me. I feel I should be cleaning his room and civilizing him. He asks why should I care whether his laundry gets done or his room is clean. I care, I yell, because I'm your goddamn mother and I'm supposed to be responsible for your fucking welfare. It's a voice in my head. Poor head, he said.

My thirteen year old descendant studies my problem. So, he says, so if I'd been around the house when Picasso tried to paint then Picasso would have turned out to be a sidewalk painter, is that about right? Consider, my male offspring, consider history. It's just possible that if Pablo Picasso had been a mother, or even a woman, she'd never have painted shit. What the hell do you think it meant to be a Spanish woman in the 19th century? Do you think she'd even have gotten out of the house (and in most places in Spain there would not even have been a sidewalk to paint), to say nothing of getting out of Spain and going to live in Paris. My son sets his jaw and says gender has nothing to do with it, a real artist never lets go of the vision. I get the feeling he means that. There are no excuses. We do what we can. The results are none of our business.

1974

I was born in 1933, the day Prohibition was repealed. It was a national holiday and nearly everyone got drunk. It was also the height of the Great Depression. I've always thought there is a distinct relationship between alcoholism and depression. A brain boiled in booze goes soft and the bottom falls out. Of course the Great Depression was the economic depression of the 1930s in which I was born, not the psychic depression of the '70s in which I live. Between that depression, the economic, and this, the psychic, there was W.W. II. Before that war, it was the money that mattered. After that, it was the mind that gave us trouble. I've been worming into the period of W.W. II during the last few years and writing poems about Dresden and Dunkirk and Hiroshima and Knossos in Crete and Nebraska and the Nile River and Calvary and Buchenwald and Britain. In Britain there was Winston Churchill and he demanded an unconditional surrender and so the war went on. Those were the years of my nymph-hood: the period between the age of dolls and the age of despair. I did not understand that the loss of my personal innocence was a national or world phenomenon as well. Oh, not that corruption and evil were anything new; only that they were happening to more people at the same time than ever before. Never before had so many suffered so much for so little, they say. Never before had there been so much collective guilt. That sort of thing. No one in particular was to blame. Not me, I don't think. Not Truman, or the scientists or the Nazis or anyone people knew about. They didn't know what the bomb would do until they tried it out. I felt the same way about the things that were happening in my life. I wanted to do it my way just to see what would happen. I did, and later on I told the story any way it suited me. I made it up, the way history is made up. If history is the collective prejudices of the ruling class at any given time, then my story is the private lie I present to the world.

Why is it then, that the world and I have come back to a sense of sin? Not that we admit it. Still I wonder why so many of us act like flagellants, beating each other to death

with explanations and protestations, always pleading inno-
cent to crimes we didn't commit. Men have tried to master
the earth and each other, and they've tried to save the earth
and help each other. We can't leave anything the hell alone.
The ancient people warned us. The artists warned us. We
eat of the tree and we die.

summer 1974

Sam and Simon and I are walking around Jewel Lake in
Tilden Park. Simon talks a lot. He asks if we remember the
winter the lake froze and the ducks slid around on their tails,
and do salamanders drown, and if Christ was a carpenter did
He make coffins and was He *really* a Jew or a red herring.
Some sweet elderly women in tennis shoes and sailor hats
ask Simon if he knows what kind of bird is the little brown
bird on the water, and he tells them it's a baby duck and
even baby ducks have trouble landing on the ice.

Sam runs into Rebecca. Rebecca is his sometimes, well if
he isn't busy, and there isn't a ball game, his sometimes-go-
and-see-her girl friend. She has a six-pack and Sam follows
her down the trail and Simon and I sit by the water. Simon
talks on about Sam and his friends and male bonding and
silver-backed gorillas leading the pack and I ask him if there
isn't more to adolescence than sex and violence and he says
of course not.

Sam comes back alone and says he wants to go and see

Godfather II and Simon has to sit down front because he talks too much. I remember my mother used to make me sit down in front.

A brown mallard hen is running along the edge of the lake. Her back is raw and several larger ducks are pecking her in a determined, impassive way. Simon grabs for the hen who seems more frightened of him than of her killers, and a band of black children appear on the path and chase the pecking ducks into the water, throwing stones after them to drive them across the lake. They yell after the ducks, "Honky motherfuckers!" Sam and Simon squeal with laughter and join them, throwing stones and screaming "Nigger cocksuckers!" They all roll on the ground together and snort with laughter.

Over pizza, Simon considers. He shakes his head and says he's no honky. A honky, he tells me, is a white male adult who drives around Harlem honking for a whore because he is too chickenshit to get out of his car and walk around asking for one. Sam says that makes a lot of sense.

Sam says the reason *Godfather* is more tragic than a western is because they used to be Romans once, they're older barbarians. Simon says no, it's the musical score which is a dirge and the movie's a funeral and that's why it's fun.

We have chocolate sundaes. Simon mutters to himself. I ask what is bothering him. He says who in the hell was the Red Baron really. He is looking at a large stuffed Snoopy doll in the ice cream parlor. I tell him I wasn't around during the First World War. Neither was I, he says, and neither were the Romans. First thing in the morning Simon is on the phone to the public library. He asks for the Red Baron's last name and he writes it down. The Red Baron, the World War I flying ace, is named Manfred Albecht Richtosen. As they used to say in the newsreels, time marches on.

summer 1974
(*I carve a limestone fossil of a god laughing at my lover*)

It happens every seven years. Transfiguration: a new self. I was thirty-three when I met him. Forty years old now and he still calls. I don't hate him, I'm just past caring. I mean seven years of one night stands with one man. I can't go on treating him like a sex object when I've forgotten where I met him. We said everything we had to say in less than a week. He's old now and cranky and paranoid and something of a bore. Rather like me. Only I don't expect undivided attention anymore. Oh, I demand it but I don't really expect it. He wants me to listen to his every word and he had nothing to say when he started. He roars a lot. I have no idea what about, but the noise impressed me for quite a while. Then it irritated me. Then I thought it was sort of sweet. And now I'm bored. Sound asleep if you want to know. If things go on this way it looks as if I might turn celibate. I'd get lots more work done. Balzac said a night in bed, in bed with a woman I mean, cost him any number of pages, I think he said eighteen. Balzac thought of it as a physical drain. For *me*, it's a brain drain. When I'm in love, I think all the time. I analyze every word, every gesture. I pick and dig for evidence of criticism or censure or even for approval. Scratch,

scratch, scratch. He quit years ago. He hears nothing. Oh, he mellows a little if I lay it on with a trowel, if I act ecstatic and gratified as hell. He basks in my afterglow. But if I'm cross or gloomy he just ignores me psychologically. Never biologically. Result: I am impassible.

Yes, it may be true the body renews itself every seven years, but brain tissue is permanent. It modifies but it doesn't renew. I only get one soul. I know this is true because when I run into people I haven't seen for twenty years I can get away unrecognized if I don't speak. If I open my mouth they hear the same old nervous system. It's my father's mother's voice I think, more than the rest. In any case, it never changes.

Perhaps it's time to quit. Time to quit talking, time to quit fucking. Gandhi quit fucking when he was thirty-seven. Seminal fluid to pituitary gland; energy turned spiritual, that sort of thing. All that heat going to the brain. For once I could get out of a male head and into my own. It's very contemporary, living alone and doing one's own thing. One's own thing. Beats getting all dressed up and spending an evening being gorgeous just for the sake of a few orgasmic moments or even for a few non-orgasmic moments. I'll give it a whirl. I'll even give it a title: Neo-Narcissism.

Cookie Crumb

All my life I've lied, made things up, made the picture fit the dream. All my life I told myself that chalk was cheese. Until, of course, it was.

April evening, 1975

I don't want to go home to an empty television set. I'll go to
La Promethea and listen to the poets. Here they are, and very
young. I feel trapped between the generations. Who isn't? This
cafe could be North Beach in the '50s, only hippies are not
beatniks, are not repeating what we were saying then.

I pin false flowers on my dress: the belladonna, deadly
nightshade; bell-shaped deep crimson flowers with glistening
black berries. I set my black hat at an angle. No one here would
recognize me if I changed my clothes. On the wall hangs a
painting of La Salamandrine, the one who passes through fire
unscathed. The portrait of Promethea smiles at her from the
poets' platform. Eastern carpets, red lantern light, an old piano,
stained-glass windows; they get me as far as the bar. With wine
before me, I consider the poets' stage: a kind of pulpit; a noose
hangs from the ceiling, twined with plastic red roses.

A poet arrives. Taking a chair to the stage, he piles his work
on the platform. The manuscripts spill. He pulls up another
chair on which he places his beer and another pile of manuscripts. His voice can be heard under a wide-brimmed hat. He
tells us he is a gay poet; his poems are printed on embossed paper;
he likes the look of the thing. He makes academic jokes which
underplay life. Wreaths of cigarette smoke come from underneath the great flat hat. The poems are about the pain of being
cast as the other woman; in his relationships he is the other
woman, with a mustache. That kind of thing. I won't call him a
derivative derelict because I liked his hat.

Another poet reads and he is gay too, he says, but he wants to be called queer. He dresses tough and reads crotch and foreskin poems. Two middle-aged straight males have wandered into the wrong bar. There is an altercation; obscene words and gestures. "Damn hippie *prev*erts." The cognoscenti demand silence for the esoteric obscenity coming from the stage. So few voices in the world and so many echoes. Who was the first original? The first caveperson to speak? In the beginning was the word and word was probably "oh, shit," and everyone everywhere said it all at once.

When the queer poet finishes he says he hopes he scared hell out of us. A black poet admonishes the audience to clap equally for each poet in turn, "cause it's all the same man, it's all the same." The same voices echoing forever.

A gang of strolling players break up the scene. They have come to perform a satire on the arrogance of poets. Terminal megalomania, narcissism and delusions of grandeur. The trouble with poets, says Julia Vinograd (Telegraph Avenue's resident poet and Bubble Lady), is nobody shoots them. One of the players, wearing a trench helmet with antlers, holds the audience captive with a burp gun and a fire hose.

Irene Dogmatic appears, wearing lace underwear and rhinestones on her rump. She admits men bring out the masochist in her. She sits with a gigantic bag between her legs. She pleads with the antlers not to have to carry this bag around with her every month. Finally she gives up and pulls the cord. The contents of the bag are dredged from between her legs: blood-soaked rags, broken baby dolls, American flags, curlers, bloodstained underpants, nylon stockings,

girdles, baskets of broken eggs, and more female flotsam all
pouring forth to the music of our national anthem.

The last poet says he hasn't anything left to say, he's said
it all. But he didn't want to go home without taking his turn,
and so he thought he would show us a little can of worms.
Each little worm should be examined in turn, he says, cause
it's all the same. Each one. Each worm. Each word.

April 1975

Everyone has written a poem about a laundromat. I feel
left out. I can't go to a laundromat on purpose. It's against
my rules for creating the found or accidental poem. It's not
right to try. At last I have to go in a laundromat to use the
phone. I look around furtively and there sits my poem: he's a
young black male sitting under the hairdryer, wearing pink
Topsy curlers in his hair. He's smoking brown cigarettes and
reading *The Letters of George Jackson*. My God, he's me.

April 1975

Why can't I get it together. Blue pencil blues: this diffi-
culty of refining and rewriting. I can't do it today — endless
adding, dangling, expanding. Reflections in the mud. Cut
crap. When in doubt, throw it out. Squeeze the essence out
of the meaning. Get rid of unnecessary references, names of

things, maps of thoughts. I'll work in one style only. I'll order a form, or form an order. But it always seems that everything is necessary to me and only always more is needed, but nothing is ever necessary except to be going on from there where it was to where is the next thing.

It's no use saying things. Necessity and memory are dry rot. Reason and psychology are excuses. Secrets of the heart are seldom news. The party line is bugged; it blocks the private vision. Doris Lessing says novels are lying nostalgia. Yes, so why not write the truth. It is not possible to write lies. Only to read them.

Blue Pencil Blues

poems are not saying
saying what is needed   is not writing
hearing is not poems
typing is not writing too
witty is not saying

simply do simply saying
each time truly
and lie when it's time for comedy
and say convention when it's time for tragedy

tragedy dies and comedy marries
and history takes all day —
so say nothing at all
as often as may be

and remember
we're not going anywhere

not this time

end of April, 1975

> *"Do you know because I tell you so*
> *or do you know do you know."*
> Gertrude Stein

Evening in the coffeehouse. Once more I am sitting here reading my notebook in which I have written that thing he said: there are only two kinds of women in the world, he said — the loved and the unloved. I make a note in the margin: Bob Benchley once said there are only two sorts of people in the world — those who divide people into two groups and those who don't.

Young women come into the cafe; Undines, sea nymphs, swimming through the smoke, floating down onto chairs as if settling on coral stools, the sand sinking down around them, marfire shining in their hair. I do not listen to their voices.

At the table in the window sits a young woman named Echo. She is a Maenad, seduced by Pan. He sits grinning at her with Saturnalian glee. She's been his to command ever since her heart broke during that fatal affair with Narcissus. It helps me to use names for things. It's why I went to school. The names of the myths help distance the pain. On bad days I call myself Cassandra. It's harmless. A young male I've known for some time sits down at my table. He makes his living stealing books, usually books on philosophy, and selling them back to the bookstores. He is listening carefully to the Undines at the next table. I ask him if he can remember the name of the woman who killed herself in Hitler's flat in

Berlin in 1931. I read somewhere she was the great love of
Hitler's life. I never doubted he had one. The young male
does not hear the question. Why am I always wringing my
hands and talking about dying, he wants to know. I only
wondered, I tell him, if she might not have changed history.
I wonder a lot about things like that. When Stalin's wife
shot herself, all Stalin said was, how could she do this to *me*,
or words to that effect. Your history is not true, the young
male says. Stalin had her killed. Everyone knows. She said
something he didn't like during a dinner party, and after he
sent her to her room he sent along someone to shoot her.

The young sea nymph sitting closest to us turns to another young woman at her table and says, well, she sure as
hell wants to get laid this evening and the young male who
steals philosophy books turns a little white and says, she
sounds awfully aggressive. I assure him she is only bored so
he turns on her and makes what would once have been
named a forward pass. A rose by any other name would
smell.

May Day 1975
(the politics of lipstick)

I'm suffering from a split lip. I've given up lipstick. It was
a political decision. Heavy. I used to wear a dark mauve:
eggplant. My lips are cracked and chapped. I'm tight-lipped,
like a dried prune. I must lie a lot or my mouth would be
relaxed, not twisted and wrinkled, bitten and bleeding.

Last night I gave a woman a hug. She took that as a political statement. The revolution of touch. Her mood changed when she saw my eyeshadow. She resented it. I can't give up my eyeshadow. I've got faded Dutch blue eyes and they disappear behind my glasses. She tells me a gob of blue eyeshadow makes a suppliant statement. Blue, she says, is pretty and appealing. I should get rid of the soft colors and use Kohl; it's charcoal and fierce.

Looking around the room, I saw she was right. I was the only woman wearing *any* make-up. When I was in high school, only liberated tramps wore make-up. Here I am again. History repeats herself.

a morning in May, 1975

There is a young woman on the subway platform. Baby on her back, baby on her lap, baby in her belly. At her age, I hadn't even made it. God bless the finger-fucking fifties.

an afternoon in May, 1975

Party line feminists overheard in coffeehouse:

— How's your vagina dear?
— Oh, my vagina's OK now I guess. How's China?
— Oh, *China*, never mind about China. I mean well, China's got her hang-ups and I've got mine.

— Oh, your vagina's in trouble then?

— I'll say. I mean even my shrink thinks I'm impenetrable.

— But he does have hope?

— Well, no. But I have Medi-Cal.

a night in May, 1975

> *"An old cunt is a dead loss."*
> Henry Miller

A young man sits in the coffeehouse, reading *The Tropic of Cancer*. "This Miller's the Messiah, man!" The young woman with him does not agree. "He's *your* poet," she says, "He doesn't speak for me."

The young man tells her Miller speaks for everyone. The poet, wrote Miller, is not one who writes verses, but someone who is capable of profoundly altering the world. That is, a messianic motherfucker like Miller! The young woman asks me if I don't think Miller was more narcissistic than messianic.

I tell them Miller was a serious artist and he made big changes. His phallocentrism is more fun than D. H. Lawrence's, if not as poetic. The young man says yes, this is because Miller rejected his mother. Lawrence loved his. That's what makes the difference, he says. If you don't reject your mother, it impedes your manhood. Impedes is the word he used.

The young woman's name is Karen. She is into poetry

and Zen. She rejects Freud and the phallocentrics. (She laughs and calls them a new rock band.) She tells the young man, whose name is Steve, that she does not recognize any difference between Platonic love and sexual love. She refuses to separate lust from love.

While Karen gets another cappuccino, Steve asks me, "Should we tell her Platonic love was Plato's love for boys? Genital sex is at the bottom of everything. I know you know that at your age. You tell her. She'll believe an older woman."

Four years is a long time trying to relate to these Berkeley poets. Futility is setting in. After Steve goes, Karen sighs and asks where is all this sisterhood she's been hearing about among women writers. Her disillusion betrays her youth. She feels poetry is no longer being written in the spiritual tradition. She loses her own faith now and Zen. Where is the sacred text to guide us? I use my Yiddish accent to tell her, "In the beginning was the *void* . . .." And the void has failed us. I pull out my notebook and show her my daily scribbles:

Impression: Involutional Melancholia,
   Paranoid Type

This is your friendly neighborhood nymphomaniac calling. Nostalgia is my thing: the fossil fragments of extinct dreams. Ezra Pound under an umbrella, sharing sandwiches with those more for-tun-ate than he. Things were more fun in the old days. Or I was.

The only good poet is a dead poet. I have no intention of dying, I shall become extinct. Back to sediment, back to primal slime, through my fossil to the bottom. Byron will lead me to the sea. (What I want to know is: *who got the brass ring?*)

I never knew a poet knew how to live. A poet is a fossil to begin with. Limestone liars make me tired. Pontificating, pretentious old pricks they are, "How unpleasant to Mr. Eliot," (not that anyone did).

No, I never knew a poet knew how to live. Dylan knew how to die: *what's he to Hecuba, nothing at all, that's why there'll be no wedding this Wednesday week way down in old Bengal.*

Listen to me love, listen just a moment. Do not speak ill of the Gentleman with the Scythe, just bring a bottle, and come at once.

Karen laughs. Is that your last word, really, she asks. Nope. This is the last.

Last List

It's all finite folks, the
orgasms and the apples,
the cars and candy bars
of a lifetime. Count them,
the books and the movies,
the operations and
adulteries, the triumphs
and trips to the seashore.

Poeta nascitur, non fit:
the poet is born, not made,
and those of us finite literary
ladies: leprechaunesses,
loveresses, prophetesses,
Ms. Fit and Ms. Unsolicited,
we're on the shelf. Didn't work out
so we didn't get in The Big Book.

Let us go then, you and I,
to sink in sorrow or in gin.
We have lingered in the trousers of our times,
by coffeehouse Lotharios abandoned and seduced
till modern poets date us and we're goosed.

June 1975

Simon has returned from a ten day intensive. His high
school (about eighty students) goes up river to a study camp
from time to time. This intensive dealt with creativity in the
various disciplines. Simon is stewing about the choice between the Dionysian and the Apollian modes of living. I, he
tells me, represent the Dionysian mode. He says I should
consider a transfer to the Apollonian life style. What's in it
for me? I ask. Well, he frowns, at least you'd get the mornings. It's true, I haven't seen the dawn in years.

July 1975

My kids are taller than I am — both of them. With tall
comes overbearing. Sam says, no he doesn't want spaghetti,
he announces, because it is full of wine, herbs, garlic, onions
and God knows what else. He says I cook this way because I
have no taste buds. He took a course at school and learned
that at my age the taste buds are dead. This from a kid who
puts ketchup on an egg. "I say it's spinach and I say to hell
with it," rings in my memory as my father's table complaints
rise in an ache of nostalgia and I think how salt hath lost its
savor.

autumn 1975

A San Francisco morning at the train station. The handwriting's on the wall: "Stephanie Stuart's a fat little hoe," and on the bench: "Stephanie Stuart is going to get hers," signed, "Pisces."

It doesn't change much, the world. Not the people. Oh, the air is changing and the water and the soil. Through the high windows I can see the pollution which covers the city. The plague of technology, the price of what men call affluence. The graffiti hasn't changed much since Rome. Since the caves! But the sea and air are full of poisons — real filth. Oh, we've learned to have more and see less. The stench of the medieval open sewer is gone, but the atmosphere's orange with death. Dead or dying though, the people never change. Here in the city by the sea, as brightness falls from the air, Stephanie is still a fat little hoe and "Harry is a homosexual," and someone, somewhere, thinks it's news.

fall 1975
(at the learning temple)

Why should I want an M.A. in creative writing. All my friends have one. I'm at San Francisco State and I have an endless cold and sore throat. I haven't been this sick since I was in college. I *am* in college. When our instructor enters the room it feels like someone just left. He tells us Theodore Roethke wrote his poems in bed. Who doesn't? The class

argues about the difference between ambiguity and ambiva-
lence. I go out for a glass of water and slip into a friend's
office and smoke some pot. I return to the classroom and
start talking.

John Donne, I pontificate, refers more than once to the
"specular stone" as a stone unknown in his own day which
the ancients had employed for building temples with trans-
parent walls. Donne found his information in a book published in 1599. I can't find it, but I believe it. Our instructor
is amused. He tries to wind up the discussion. He says it's
time to wind up and get down to the matter at hand. The
matter at hand is a serious assignment on John Donne and
the metaphysical poets. He explains that once I really get
into it, I'm sure to enjoy it.

I know the ancients could see through stone. Stoned or
sober, all I see is school. I'll learn. Send not to know for
whom the bell tolls, find out who tolls it.

September 1975

The lunch wagon at San Francisco State: I buy a liverwurst
sandwich. Sitting on a bench, I pick a camellia and put it in
my hat. A young woman sees me do this. Quickly she asks if
she may sit with me. She asks if I believe in God. She says I
seem to be enjoying my sandwich and I look as if I might eat
it all. The bitch wants my sandwich. She talks about how
she and her dog have been in town for three days and how

beautiful everything is here in California but Californians
don't appreciate what they've got. The half-eaten liverwurst
sandwich sits in my lap. I put it down on the bench and
smile my idiot smile, asking the young woman if she really
thinks it's true there are no lesbians in Russia. Walking
away, I can't help looking back to see. Her little dog eats the
whole thing.

end of September, 1975

Noon at the Bay Area Rapid Transit station. I sit on the
bench and look toward the Berkeley hills. The hills are
green. Two pigeons fly down from the sky. They soar through
the open roof of the station in a great arc, curving into the
glass windows leading to the green hills. I expect the glass to
shatter but there is only a dull thud. One bird falls, limps,
lurches, and drops quietly, head falling softly to one side.
The other writhes in a furious flap of wings, her feathers
flying, twisting in agony as if her back were broken.

A woman sitting on my right says well how stupid can
you get. She says she thought pigeons were smarter than
that. In a final desperate lurch, the broken bird falls off the
platform across from us, landing on the train rails.

A woman sitting on my left, a woman with shellacked
hair and eyelashes glued tight, says well it was probably a
male chasing a female and serves them both right.

October 1975

My old friend Julia insists we go to our twentieth college reunion. She has a sadistic streak. So-and-so, she says, is dying of cancer. I don't remember so-and-so and this doesn't seem like the right reason for a class reunion but I've forgotten how the bourgeoisie live and I decide to go and see. Julia and I went to a girls' college. Private, arty, and expensive.

We drive to the Piedmont hills. I've pinned myself together in my poet's drapery; black shawls and hat and red feathers. Julia is chic and svelte and she is hurt by my feathers. She smokes furiously, with a Bette Davis flourish. When she gets all dressed up, she starts acting like a female impersonator.

We arrive at the Alpine Circle in Piedmont, the home of Dr. and Mrs. Tong. I cannot remember the name of Mrs. Tong who was in my graduating class in 1955 so I have to call her Mrs. Tong. Haute bourgeois: four bathrooms, indoor pool, several sunken TV pits, rumpus room, the works.

Most surprising is the age of the people. There are rooms full of middle-aged and even old persons. The best-looking man in the room is pouring the drinks. Julia and I had promised ourselves to stay sober, but I can't handle reality. After several bourbons, the man pouring the drinks remembers he went out with me the night he met his wife. This reduces him to maudlin tears. After that it's all a Celtic blur. There's a woman who still wears her hair in a style that doesn't look like a hat. She once stole a man I don't remember really wanting but I didn't want him stolen. I ask her if she remembers what a wicked femme fatale she was and so promiscuous and her father a clergyman and all. She has had a lot to drink and she tells me that was only because she was impotent as a young woman and had no orgasms until she was thirty-seven. None, not even of any kind. She says I've done better because I have a space between my teeth and that means I'm sensual. It's a rumor that got started in Johannesburg. About the teeth, not about me. She asks me about the dates of my first orgasms. I tell her I can't remember and she thinks I'm showing off. I tell her I remember stopping off at a gas station on the way home from school when I was ten. What a shame, she says. Not shame, privacy is the issue, I explain. She cries a little because her daughter is a poet like me and no one loves her daughter because she has a size 38D cup. She means that other *girls* don't love her daughter which is just as well I think.

Julia is as tight as I am. She is deep in conversation with a woman who is saying to her that if their friendship is to be revived it will have to be on the basis of mutual respect this time. Anyone who knows my friend Julia knows she suffers from terminal superiority (it's her animus, for the Jungians) and anyone who truly loves her must put up with it. She knows what's right. She's consumed with conviction. I launch a drunken defense. Julia looks as if she might throw me in the pool. I tell her my threshold for insult is too high for her. She announces it's time to get what's-her-face (me) home and she drags me out trailing feathers, both of us dead drunk. We talk on the same bumble-booze-brainless wave length. Great friendship in our hearts, of course, while she rages about the Tongs and the middle classes. She seethes with socialism and red righteousness and I try to contribute, Marx-wise. Then she tells me what a fool I am to love men who don't give me money. I ask her how old she was when she had her first orgasm and she takes me to the Pup Hut and orders coffee.

In the morning I discover I've lost my little black notebook. It's in one of the Tongs' bathrooms. I call and Mrs. Tong is Kim and the notebook is in her desk and she says nothing. Perhaps she didn't read it. All during the evening I'd kept hiding in a bathroom and writing notes about the people. There was the chunky set in the living room sitting in a circle around the food. I dipped in and out of the room to throw a fish into the conversation and get back the bait. A red-faced bellicose male barked at me, "Are you some kind of feminist?"

"Isn't everyone?" I asked.

"You must have known my wife," he hollered.

I might have known his wife once, before the flood. I might even have known Kim, or the woman without any orgasms, or the man who met his wife, but it's too long ago now and those people died.

"Never, I assure you, never in the biblical sense." I kissed the red-faced man and he grinned and kissed me back.

20 November 1975
(*for whom the bell tolls*)

Well, Mother, Franco's dead today. Ding dong, the old man's dead. He should have died heretofore; about forty years heretofore. Mother died so long ago. Franco outlived her thirty years. He was not one of her favorite people. She was a parlour pink; a watered-down Red. Picasso's *Guernica* hung in our pink parlour; Hemingway's hat in the hall (or his muddy boots or something). I was given crib notes on the Civil War in Spain. Of course I don't really remember; I thought the axis were axes . . . I hadn't learned to read. Francisco Franco was a fascist, Mother Fucker, you name it. I knew she wished him dead. I heard about the blood boot and the people's war. We were for the people of course. She read all about it and talked to all the other women and they said the same. They knew about feudal and they knew about fascist.

It's too late to matter, but he's dead now at last. I'll play Ophelia and Lady Macbeth for you Mother:

He is dead and gone, lady, he is dead and gone. Pray you mark. Who would have thought the old man to have had so much blood in him. Had he not resembled my father as he slept, I had done the deed.

Who was it said, the world won't be the same without Big Daddy, or else perhaps it will.

November 1975

Time to write my annual autumn autopsy. Every year I go underground before the winter solstice. I try to get it together, wrap it up, recycle it. Like the ground hog I hide in a hole and then I crawl out and look around, only in my case, I'm always waiting for winter; and when I peek out to check the weather, that is, the people and the scene, well if I see my shadow I just get drunk. That's how I know it's still fall and the year isn't dead yet. I'm coming out very slowly this year. There's still a little shadow that goes in and out with me. I don't think I'll finish in time for the dark. Of course, it isn't hard once you get started. The first thing is to get "it" all laid out before you. Then there must be a clean knife and a clear vision. Before consulting the entrails it's necessary to do a lot of deep breathing because of the smells. This year I must say the auspices weren't very auspicious. I threw away the heart and that tiresome burden I see in the mirror. I set aside several strands of my nervous system. With these I can begin.

First, I write down everything I know, which doesn't take long. Then I type everything on those little index cards. I underline all the political stuff in red. I use a blue highlighter for all the personal parts. I distinguish the fact from the fiction by using the scissors to cut the corners. At some point I take a psychotic break which usually lasts three days although I have no way of knowing for sure. Then I carefully reread everything and select the really heavy stuff, profoundly engrave it on a stone tablet, bake it, break it, and smash it all to fragments. I then mail the dust to the *Atlantic Monthly*: "The Sands of Mind" will be this year's title.

December 1975
(. . . *The Piltdown Woman meets the worm*)

Late last night I finished my paper on William Blake: "Oh rose, thou art sick." Mutability, death, and the rest of it. I finished my brandy and went to bed.

In the early morning dark, in the faintest light, I see something moving on my hand. I am not really awake. The thing looks blackish. It crawls toward the third finger of my left hand and bites my skin delicately but with a piercing strength. I lurch upright and smash my hand against the bed, grabbing for the light. I search the quilt to find the terrible thing which made me think I might be dead, after all, and the worms e'en at me. I find a grey-green worm oozing near my pillow; curled and cringing and hungry. There is a yellow spot where I smashed it. Roses in a ceramic pot beside my pillow . . . crimson and white, tucked into mint leaves, overblown and the petals falling in a little puddle on the night table. Looking deep into the blossom, I find another worm. I pick the pair of them up with toilet paper and flush them away, throwing the roses in after them. I rinse the glazed pot and throw the mint out the window into the trees. I throw the bedding in the bathtub until I can wash it and hang it in the sun. I handle it as if it were contaminated with lice or bedbugs. I had bedbugs once, in New York, years ago. It was a joke then. I waited with soft soap to catch them when they crept out after dark. I had to have proof to force the landlord to call the exterminators. Now I shudder at the thought of things crawling on me while I sleep. Looking at my hand, I feel the intense bite again. I am meat. I am edible. Curled up in a clean blue sheet, I shiver and try to go back to sleep. I get a sleeping bag out of the closet and bury myself in it, trying to feel bundled and safe. It's four in the morning. Rosey, thou art sick, old girl. When I was young and twenty, I was not afraid of anything living or dead. Tonight I'm terrified. I dream of empty seas and dry sand, cracked mud and ashes of roses, sandstone faces of desert lovers. I hear the gentleman with the scythe calling on the night wind, "I'm coming Rosey, stay for me." Well, hell. I'll be smart. I'll be cremated. No conqueror worm, only trans-figuration. An urn of ashes on a shelf. Myself, Madame Pavlova, an endless number of Romans, Jews, Vikings . . . all burned alive or dead. Very dignified dust.

To keep from dreaming, I get out my tape recorder. The worm bringeth forth the word. I begin with a dedication to Eddie Poe: "All I loved, I loved alone." He, too, wrote about his nightmares. Drank himself to death. Afraid of being buried alive. Who isn't?

I wake up suddenly in a clammy sweat. The tape recorder has run on alone, recording my alpha waves. I reverse it to where I fell asleep and try to record my last nightmare.

In the dream there seemed to be a sort of mausoleum. It is cold there and I am trying to sleep on a slab. I begin to think it would have been better to have been buried in the sun. I pull the blankets closer around my shoulders; the blanket is a linen shroud. There is a boy there, lying dead under a sheet; only he is not dead any more than I am. The air is dank and the stones are grey. Sam and Simon seem to be with me. They ask for information. Data. Simon says it looks like Juliet's tomb. Sam says it's a dump and he wouldn't live here with his dog. He goes out to play frisbee. I try to remember Juliet and I form the words: "If all else fail, myself have power to die," but I cannot speak aloud and Simon is laughing at me. He larks around like a Noel Coward song, singing, "A tomb with a view and you . . . .." I tell him to hush up and behave himself. I make mother noises and Simon dances off, making an obscene gesture and saying "This is for you," another obscene gesture, "and this is for your horse." I can see the hand of the boy whose body is framed underneath the sheet. The hand is greenish-grey and puffy plump. The fingers crawl onto the sheet and pull it off. Then he jumps up and wraps the sheet around him as if he were in a Turkish bath. He is too fat to be Sam or Simon. He goes to a man who is his doctor and he says that what I deserve is to be reincarnated as a giraffe and go through a lifetime without a voice box. He grins at me and says, "squeak, squeak." Suddenly I can speak and I insist this boy is dead. The boy yells, "No, I'm adopted, I'm adopted." I argue about all this with the doctor who I know to be an absolute phony. One of his eyes is black; charcoal is running down the side of his face instead of tears. He finally states that as far as he can tell the boy is alive. I had known this all along but the boy's lack of self-awareness bothered me. He is acting like a primal animal spirit. He is Pan; Jesus is not yet born. If I can get rid of the doctor, I can find out the truth. Although the boy is not my son, I can plot with him. I promise him a six-pack if he will get rid of the doctor. He begins to talk, telling the doctor all about Sir Thomas Crapper who invented the flush toilet in England and how the doughboys went over in

World War I and came home saying, "Got to go to the crapper," and he goes on about the English and their watercloset jokes and the doctor looks at me knowing it is my fault the boy talks all the time and then I am the boy's mother but she is not me. I am the mother of Sam and Simon. The woman who is the mother of this boy dances on a stone slab. She is wild as wind. Things turn around. Confusion and displacement and a ledge at the end of the tomb which is a subterranean cave. We are near the edge of a precipice which is precarious and slippery. Moss, lichen and the usual mist can be seen as the earth quakes and the tremor causes me to reach for the hand of the boy who is mine now and I show him the end of the world. Vast floating cities pass before us; whole civilizations, ancient villages, rivers and seas in which the stones at the bottom of the water appear to be junkyards of industrial waste or crushed cars, all covered by clear and luminous mountain streams — now and then sea birds swimming to the surface and flying to meet us. At last we can see the time to come: a sort of movie Atlantis in the future where everything is self-contained and there are no connecting wires. Illumination comes from fireflies in the air and from phosphorescent sea creatures. This phosphorescence, I tell the boy, is marfire, the light which comes from the depths of the sea.

I record my dream on tape. It is almost dawn. I describe the outline, fragments, slivers, and a space opening into eternity.

Words. I get the dictionary and look up "nightmare." "I will ride thee o'nights like the mare." Hum. Sexist. Anyway *mara* is an incubus, and somehow akin to sanskrit meaning "he crushes." Also: 1) A kind of spirit or goblin, or fiend that sits on your chest when you're asleep; 2) Melancholy, the blue devils, the blues; 3) A hag, witch or specter. Reading further I find the plural is Maria; the sea, or a pool, or the dark of the moon (once thought to be the seas of the moon or the seas of Mars now thought to be vegetation but of course they're really seas). I can't stop reading dictionaries. The labyrinth of language. I have a dictionary in my bed that outweighs my last lover. Words without frames, without a context. So fragmented. How free they are. Margaret is a pearl. Short form is Greta. There's my answer.

I will go to visit my friend Greta who lives at Aptos by the sea. I will tell her I forgot to be buried in the sun. I will tell her the worm is real and Rosey, thou art sick, and I eat death every day. Doesn't everyone, she will say. Duck soup, she will say, and oh yes the dark night of the soul, and let's go downtown and look in the shops and go to that new bar with old lanterns; the Belladonna Bar by the sea. "Bella donna: Deadly nightshade. A night-walking prostitute." Death and sex.

Hum. Tape recorder on again. Title of the next fragment: *The Piltdown Woman*. See references to the Piltdown Man, found in East Sussex, England. A supposedly very early primitive modern man based on skull fragments uncovered in a gravel pit at Piltdown and then used in combination with comparatively recent skeletal remains of various animals in the development of an elaborate fraud. Widely accepted at first, this skull, assembled by a man, was discovered to be a fake. Elsewhere described as an extinct prehistoric being, also known as "Dawn Man," a genus of early Pleistocene primate, essentially human, but later held invalid as a genus because of doubt *as to the exact relation of all fragments.* That's me all right. Free association has blown my mind. All those sea slime dreams have destroyed me. Just another fraud. As the Piltdown Woman I can really get my teeth into the truth. Perverse and put-down, my existence is denied. A pastiche of worn out words, he said once. I'm accused of cleverness as if it were a sin. She is merely clever, they say. I sacrifice wisdom for wit, let profundity go for a pun. Could be. Sometimes I'm rolling forward with a tidal wave of words and just as I'm about to break I reverse the image like a movie going backwards. It all becomes absurd as the wave rolls right back where it came from, or it freezes in the air and so I end there on a facetious note. Cut my own throat. Pull the rug out from under the . . . there, I've destroyed the integrity of the image cluster. Do I care what people say? Am I phony? Isn't all art a lie? Like the Piltdown person, art's a real fake. Like me. Once I told my kindest teacher I wanted to be a Renaissance woman. I was eighteen. She laughed until she choked and called me a phony phony.

I doze off again. I dream I am sleeping in a borrowed bed. In my hand I am clutching some coins, some change. The change is left over from the last drink I bought for myself in the Belladonna Bar near the River Styx before coming here to this place which is now. I am sleeping with the one I am most used to but he is not the one I thought he was. The balcony has no railing. One side of the house is not connected to the other side. There are two staircases; separate

entrances. I'm too tired to wake up. My eyes burn. If I close
them more night terrors will come. I see actors on a stage
moving like dolls. They move but they are not breathing. I
ask them what makes the wave stop and the film run backwards. Do I do that or does it go by itself? Did I learn it? Is it
a conditioned response? One of the actors comes forward
smiling. The actor is an old lover who tormented me in bed.
What a shock to see his lying grin. He always went into
reverse and swam backwards whenever the wave crested in
me. It's getting light outside. I remember setting out at
midnight, leaving home and crossing the desert, traveling to
the seashore, arriving in the early morning of my childhood.
I was three the first time I left home in the dark, driving from
Tucson to La Jolla. The desert is cool at night. I hear the surf
which is the voice of my mother as we drive past the row of
palm trees which lead down the hill. I smell the seaweed, the
mist, the iodine kelp. Perhaps I'm still sleeping. I could sleep
until I die.

Time to get on with it. The river of life, the course of
events; I search for my hands and face so I can eat breakfast.
People are bleeding to death on the radio, the blood running
out of the speaker and down on my bedsheets. The folk
songs of Chilean martyrs get me as far as the shower. The
bathtub fills up with blood. I try to look at the barracks
where I live and say the words they taught me; the words I
keep trying to swallow but which stick in my throat and I
cannot vomit up my guilt and I cannot swallow my terror.
There is my super-ego looking at me from my mirror, saying
again, how can you worry about yourself when thousands are

screaming their last? You are guilty of guilt. How can I love you, Rosey, old girl? Love must be earned with tears and blind suffering and you have not suffered enough, never *can* suffer enough in one lifetime to leave a mark as big as a pee-hole in the antarctic. River blindness has not struck you down; there is no little black fly at the corner of your eye. You have not walked naked into the gas chambers in the death camp to shield your child from the last terror in the dark. You have never held in your fist the fragment of stone soap they gave the prisoners going to the poison showers. You have not walked down to the sea and set forth a lantern upon the water to sail out to the soul of your father burnt to a shadow at Hiroshima. You have no share in these things. You have not even been permitted to suffer hard enough to know yourself. You sad survivor, telling tales to tape, how can I go on living with you? Still, once more, so breakfast can continue to continue, I forgive you, old woman, and I wish you roses sick or roses well.

Having showered and had my orange juice, I put on my new ice blue nightgown and bury myself in the sleeping bag once more. I look at the William Blake poem on the cover of my English paper:

The Sick Rose

O Rose, thou art sick!
The invisible worm
That flies in the night,
In the howling storm

Has found out thy bed
Of crimson joy,
And his dark, secret love
Does thy life destroy.

I'm damned if I'll lose any sleep over insomnia. I tuck
Willie Blake under the bed and sink down deeper in the
sleeping bag. Faintly I hear Sam say to Simon, "Well, she
looks embalmed, let's go to the doughnut shop before she
wakes up."

noon the same day . . .

Sam and Simon come home from the doughnut shop
with glazed jelly rolls. Within walking distance of our apartment there is not only a doughnut shop, but a Taco Bell,
Sizzler, Red Barn, Kentucky Fried Chicken, Straw Hat Pizza,
Copper Penny, Foster's Freeze, Chicken Delight, Jack-in-
the-Box, McDonald's, Fish and Chips, Caspers, and The
Pup Hut. I pontificate to my bored children about junk food,
about the general malaise, about television, about what

Philistines they are, about their media minds, about the integrity of the image cluster, until Sam tells me I'm a pain in the brain and splits to visit his girl friend. Sam's girl friend is a vanilla blonde this year. She cooks for him.

I look in my mirror at Lilith, she who destroys her demon children. I get Sam and Simon mixed up with the world. Like a cannibal mama mouse, the more they argue the faster I eat them. They are part of the patriarchy whether they will or no. Male chauvinist piglets? Baby machos. Sam will always find a woman to feed him. He deserves it.

Simon asks if I'm enjoying my suffering. He says if there were no suffering, it would be necessary for me to invent it. He calls me a megalomasochist — sacred cow and suffering mama. I pick up a copy of *The Hite Report* and throw it at his head. He exits, laughing.

I sit on the floor, fuming and frustrated. Where else in the world, or in history, would a woman in her forties, going into menopause, be the guardian and guide of two emerging adolescent males? I try to sit calmly and get a grip on myself. I'm the adult.

After awhile I hear little popping sounds coming from Simon's guitar. Maybe it's trying to tell me something. Maybe it's haunted. Finally I go and examine it, turning it over and shaking it. A spoonful of Simon's Mexican jumping beans fall in my lap.

Christmas, 1975

Sam has decided he likes older women. He says they have brains. *Mea culpa*. Actually he likes them because he's lazy and they don't giggle. Embittered and twenty, they know the score. The current one is very pretty, very soft. Beware my son, I tell him, beware of vanilla blondes who glow in the dark.

Turns out she isn't old enough for him after all. One night he comes home exasperated. Why, he wants to know, why is it all these women talk about is babies? Well, I tell him, if you don't know that yet then your sex education has been something of a flop. Hell, he protests, one thing doesn't have to lead to another.

New Year's Eve, 1975

On New Year's Eve I always consider giving up the grape. I consider and then I reconsider. My excuse is my conviction that drinking goes with scribbling. It's an old trick: Elizabeth Barrett was a junkie; that kind of thing.

What *were* they drinking, all the literati . . . all poets are lushes but not all lushes are poets. We've had a few sober poets, and any number of sober writers although not in Ireland (with the notable exception of George Bernard Shaw who was perhaps pure spirit and so didn't need any).

This evening after a cup of wine I began to think in simple similes: the writer *as* a drink.

Henry Miller as dark beer with a chaser. Thomas Mann as after dinner brandy on an empty stomach. Anais Nin as a strong sweet distilled liqueur. That sort of thing.

Then I had another cup of wine and I began to *see* them drinking . . . and sometimes why . . .

Jane Austen sipping lemon tea with minted leaves and sometimes looking out the window into the trees . . .

Colette swallowing sweet breakfast chocolate . . . absinthe stains on the bedside table . . . an aperitif in the afternoon on the sly in a cafe he never frequents . . .

Virginia Woolf out for a treat but only once a week a long walk first and then scones to go with . . .

George Sand smoked the little cigars first, then she drank a few sips of whatever he was pouring . . . later watering it down so she could write while he slept . . .

Sigrid Undset drank the mead of the medieval myth like the Nordic maiden she was . . . Catholic to the core . . . the wafer and the wine. (My old friend Jake says she's a bore so I told him to go take a flying leap in the fjord, after all didn't she win the Nobel Prize for Literature in 1928, and Jake said oh, the only time I tried to read her stuff hell I thought she was an *historian* . . .)

George Eliot took tea with the usual toast but no liquor left when the party's over . .. he drank of course but finally only when she did and it was love without marriage no fooling.

Then I had another cup of wine and I got a little lurid. A 19th century storm was raging. I opened the windows and looked out over the moors and there they were: the Victorian ghosts, the Christian souls. Muttering *mea culpa, mea culpa*, I felt an acute attack of brontephobia coming on. Now the name Bronte means thunder and brontephobia is the fear of thunder and lightning but of course it's *them* I'm afraid of. Heathcliff and the rest. Once in my dreams, Emily stood slicing the tomatoes she threw at me. She took the largest slice from the center and dropped it over her head; all the seeds turned to gemstones and the wet red swam around her in a cloak. The laughter of Pan poured from her throat. Still dreaming, I ran until I fell into the lurid mist of that third watercolor Jane Eyre showed to Mr. Rochester. I was drowning in the sea of that picture, reaching for the gold bracelet around the neck of the black cormorant. I woke up drenched in sea salt sweat. Oh, for my sake, Charlotte, could you (at least in my dreams) take a real drink like a simple Irishman and put away the spirits of ammonia and treacle sin syrup laced with hot chocolate desire.

Emily Bronte died in 1848 at the age of 29. I think she drank hemlock. Straight. Anne Bronte died the next year, when she too was 29, asking to be taken to Scarborough because she'd never seen the sea. They buried her there instead of at Haworth parsonage . . . so she does not walk night after night the way the others do. Charlotte lived to be 39. She died of phthisis (tuberculosis) and pregnancy.

Time to go for a walk. Walked to the store in the rain. Bought another bottle of burgundy. Got out my list.

Ernest Hemingway: Bourbon on the rocks I suppose. What do I know. Whatever he was drinking, it wasn't *that* that killed him.

F. Scott Fitzgerald: The drink that fires the dream . . . and burns the body alive.

Dylan Thomas: Beer for breakfast and any and everything else. Never took coffee or tea. Bitters all day and real booze when the work was done.

Anais Nin: Thimbles of disparate distilled liqueurs each day in her diary. Wine at formal places in gardens of prose poems. Blood if needed. Blood for lovers who couldn't, never would, or shouldn't, drink.

Gertrude Stein preferred food to drink, serving alphabet vegetable soup for an entree and beef tenderloin for those who eat words. Cakes and plum brandy for those who stay till the end . . . Melanctha was one of three . . . *Each One As She May* . . . and Alice.

Sylvia Plath . . . thistles, and yes, she drank them.

Isak Dinesen . . . time and the history of the heart of ancient woman . . . she could smell the sea of Africa before the land rose.

Toni Morrison . . . "pack up all your cares and woes . . . bye, bye, black bird" . . . there was a time, she says, when Africans could fly. This was a time before salt. There are words for women, she says. There are ways to know a whore is a lover, a servant is a laborer, and a mammy is a mother. Laughter and jungle red wine. Black women, she says, seem less alone. Look at literature: *Anna Karenina* has no woman friend to trust. *Madame Bovary* had no auntie to straighten her out. All the way to that Irish trash, Scarlet O'Hara, white women in books seem to be going about the business of the acquisition of a male or males and, of course, they're damned if they get 'em and damned if they don't. Toni writes *now* as it comes out of *then* . . . black woman wisdom doesn't divide.

Joseph Conrad drank the salt from the sea and never set foot on land again. "Mistah Kurtz — he dead."

D. H. Lawrence . . . wine and wine and wine and wine and more of
that . . . but well drunk for a dying man.

T. S. Eliot . . . dandelion wine, dearie, laced with the blood of the lamb.

Time to pour again. I hope someone's counting my drinks.

Elizabeth Barrett drinking her tea laced with laudanum; the wine of opium. The wine of love and leisure with an Englishman of letters and off to Italy for baroque. She went to visit George Sand; Elizabeth taking note that although she did not observe Madame Sand to smoke, it was, however, deeply to be regretted that Madame Sand surrounded herself with so many persons of the "ragged red or lower theatrical" types.

Mary Shelley could have used a drink. Nothing could mask the odor of death in her life, the child stillborn and all those she loved either dead or monsters, or both.

Christina Rossetti drowned deep in the holy water at the font. Then sips from her brother Dante Gabriel's unholy cup: belladonna, belladonna, deadly nightshade, a spiritual opium at last, in the garden of Solomon where she slept alone ...

Dorothy Parker drank gin from a flask in the ladies room and mixed drinks in public at cocktail parties with her heart tucked inside her handbag, sealed in a plastic wrap.

Edna St. Vincent Millay drank wine from his grapes when he was around, but she carried her own flask and she traveled.

Emily Elizabeth Dickinson drove herself from drink, insisting thought could think, until at last she fell in love with death; the sweetest drunkard we can know . . .

And one last time I reach for the wine. The year is done and temperance has not touched me.

"Come, fill the cup . . .
The Bird of Time has but a little way to fly
and Lo! the Bird is on the Wing."
(Rubaiyat)

Sappho drank the Aegean Sea in one long lost song.

John Donne, quite undone by his dear dead wife, Anne Donne*, swallowed his pride and published.

*Anne Moore married John Donne in 1601. She was 17. She died at the age of 33. She had borne her husband 12 children, of whom seven survived her.

Sartre, sweet Jean Paul, drank every and nothing at all, insisting they were both the same. Samuel Beckett: the bone of the existential echo, drinks the desert dry, a nihilist in love, no sweat.

I suppose I should mention the old man last:

"Oh Churl! Drunk all, and left no friendly
drop to help me after?
I will kiss thy lips;
Haply some poison yet doth hang on them,
To make me die . . .."
(Romeo and Juliet
Act V, scene iii)

January 1976

Oh, to live in little Albany, here on the edge of Berkeley, in this bicentennial year. Simon has run up an American flag (only 48 stars) on his television aerial. Someone in town has painted all the fireplugs red, white and blue. In Albany, even the dogs get a bicentennial minute.

1976
(an honored name)

They've dug up Betsy Ross. A very important woman this year. At first they couldn't find her, so they dug up a graveyard and unearthed lots of her relatives. They found her at last and they identified the bones and they were the real ones.

Later they found a new place to bury her where the public can pay money to visit her grave.

1976

It is a comfort to look in the mirror this morning and consider that, decadent as I am and weary as I have become, if I had had my way and managed to marry the great love of my seventeenth year, I would now be the wife, and doubtless the drunkard wife, of the President of the Junior Chamber of

Commerce in a California beach town run by a den of
Republicans.

God save us all from what we want.

fall 1976

"Poor child, what have they done to you?"

*(This phrase is found in the notebooks of Sigmund Freud. It dates
from the early years when he still believed in the reality of sexual
abuse. In later years, he came to reject his first impression and to
believe that women imagined abuse because they desired it. This
could do little but increase their hysterical symptoms.)*

Thinking of Kay. Remembering how she shocked us. So
ribald and Rabelaisian, saying how foreplay bored her, she'd
rather get right down to it. Standing nude in front of the
mantel mirror in that Manhattan apartment in the winter of
1957, plucking the black hairs that curled around her nipples,
saying she'd found a man who could keep it up all weekend.

Remembering her at fifteen, in the dark hall of her house
in Santa Monica. Her mother small too, and stiff with
arthritis, too tired to do the dishes, too depressed to talk. Kay
saying she'd promised her Mom to clean up the house after
school. She picked up a few newspapers, put some dishes to
soak in the rusty sink, went to the door of her mother's
bedroom and brusquely demanded money to go out.

Twirling around on the seat at the drugstore fountain,

she said she had better tell me about her mother if I was going to come over again. Her mother had been raped seven years ago. It happened one evening on the beach. Since then, her Mom never leaves the house alone. It was sad and all, but her father couldn't deal with it so he left them the year after it happened. It was real important that no one hear about it at school because her mother imagined everyone knew and talked about it, and they couldn't afford to move. I promised not to tell. In fact, I forgot.

Over all these years, bumping into Kay, she was always in search of the infinite fuck, the phallic solution, the existential stranger on Camus' beach, the last man on earth. Once or twice she thought she'd found him. She'd disappear for a year or so, then pop up in some unlikely bar, explaining that she needed to meet someone new. Someone who wasn't hung up, someone who wasn't afraid of sex.

Once she asked what I got out of motherhood. Did I wash my little boys' peckers? Did they have big peckers and did I take them to the beach? Bury them in the sand? No kids for her, thank God, she said, and no house with dishes and damp. She bought me a drink though, the year my eldest son started high school. She said I shouldn't live with my sons, not now that they were big. We had a few harsh words; even I get sick of sickness from time to time.

Then today, after an absence of two years, she surfaced in Berkeley, sitting alone at a table in the cafe. She had a black eye and the shakes. Her hair was dyed jet black. She pretended she didn't know me and I pretended back.

January 1977

> *"In the true dark night of the soul,*
> *it is always three o'clock in the morning:*
> *day after day after day."*
>   F. Scott Fitzgerald

Time dies. I used to think I would go mad. I've given that up. I'll remain lucid until it's over. I might die sleeping. That would be nice. I've tried to escape the knowledge of myself by following threads through labyrinths; I've come to the end of that rope. Nothing left to die for me, except time.

I beg myself to get on with it. I spend hours considering whether or not to take ten minutes' exercise. I worry for days and weeks about an assortment of dog-eared paperback books; whether to store them, give them away, take them to the used bookstore, leave them alone on buses, bury them near the trees. I have in my closet a stack of old *Theatre Arts* magazines from the 1920s, '30s, and '40s, which I've carried with me from apartment to apartment for twenty years, meaning to look at them again some day. I finally decided to give away a huge box of old clothes from the '50s, only a year before they came back into style. One moment I want to preserve everything; fill a museum with the flotsam and jetsam of a lifetime. The next moment I want to burn the house down and start all over with a robe, a bowl, and a new felt pen.

Someday I will get my apartment arranged the way I want it. Answer all the letters. Dust everything. Make the phone call I've put off for seventeen years. I have kept all the

poems ever written to me. They sit in a blue box in my top
drawer. I can't throw them away until I look through them
once more.

   I lie in bed for days staring at the face on the ceiling,
trying to remember what thing is most important to do. I
carry an overdue library book around in my bag for months.
I have filed Christmas cards for more than ten years, throwing away a few more each time, sorting the others, answering
one.
   My friends tell me I dwell on death. They should know. I
should try to change. I should attempt psychotherapy. I am
advised to go out and circulate. I must be out-going. I should
get out. I should go for a walk in the sun. I'll go.
   It is midnight on the street. I should have waited for the
light. On the corner is an antique store with windows full of
time. Inside the window, a black cat glides carefully through
the crystal, the old lace, the catatonic 19th century dolls.
She rubs against the legs of ancient love seats, jumps down
from a silenced clock and slips inside a musty wardrobe
cupboard. That's enough circulation.
   Back inside the apartment, it's still hours until morning.
I could take a nap. If I get plenty of rest I'll feel better. My
liver is scarcely functioning, I stay in bed so much. I'm crazy
for sleep. I'll take anything for sleep.
   The sleeping pill wears off by evening. I must go out. I
must see people. See the people. See the twilight people in
the coffeehouse. Quick, yell at the people before they yell at
me. Talk them up the wall and shout them shut. If I stop
talking, even for a moment, one of them will get me. I am

very outgoing.

I talk for hours to keep from saying anything. I do remarkably little harm. That can be said: She did not do a great deal of harm. A little here and there to this one and that one but less and less as time went on. It is not that I am unsocial. Certainly it is not that. I can rise to an occasion. I become quite high, even manic, when I am among my fellows. I don't of course listen to them, but I hear everything. I cannot shut it out. Alone in my room their words leak in through the cracks and around the frames of the windows. They're easier to listen to when it rains. Most of the time their voices are only echoes in the air and their faces float in a sort of Celtic cesspool at the bottom of a well, an occasional corpse surfacing, grinning and grey . . .

I am still sitting at the table in the coffeehouse. "Eye contact," the man shrieks at me. He wants me to look him in the eyes. Barbarian. In the East it is understood that a glance is the most personal communication. Anyone can touch in the dark. It's the optic nerve that sears the soul; the look that lasts. I pull myself together and look at him hard. He disappears in smoke. I don't have to do that much anymore. They leave me alone for the most part. I pass for mad. These confrontations, eyeball to eyeball, rape the spirit and leave me shattered. I don't even want to see them when they call on the phone.

And so, if they let me alone now, at last, finally I'll scatter the ashes of my self; falling from so abstract a summit they touch no one . . . becoming memories so brief they melt as softly as spores sinking into the earth . . . returning always to themselves . . . as rain might wash the sea.

autumn 1977

In the coffeehouse we talk quietly. Around the table, we talk to ourselves. Early in the morning, in this smoke filled room, we make remarks to give each other the impression we exist. Only two sorts of people left in our world: the ignorant and the terrified.

Crossing the street to the bookstore, I see a young male sitting on the curb with his head in his hands. His T-shirt says: "Reading Rots the Mind." He picks a flower from the gutter and gives it to the girl crouched behind him. She smiles and touches his face, laughing suddenly. Holding his head still with one hand, she carefully picks a fighting crab louse from his eyebrow. She puts it down on the sidewalk with reverence. I give them spare change, telling myself they confirm my existence.

winter 1977

> *"When I am dead my dearest*
> *Sing no sad songs for me*
> *Plant thou no roses at my head*
> *Nor shady cypress tree."*
>   Christina Rossetti

I went to visit my old friend and teacher. We were together in the theatre in the old days and she is dying now. She went to Russia and saw Chekhov's house; everything is so beautiful she says she cannot believe she's leaving it behind. She says she will have a pink satin coffin and she drinks codeine cocktails over chipped ice and she is still waiting, sweet goodnight lady, waiting for love to come. Soon she says, soon she will be sleeping in her pink satin coffin and now she is, now she is.

I can't sleep in this heat wave. In dreams I hear the cypress trees above me. Simon is fourteen now and puberty has come and he doesn't sleep very well either. Late last night he woke up and wandered outside, goofy from the heat. He circled the apartment house pool a few times; standing at the deep end he spread his arms out crying: "They never learn, not Christ, not nobody!" as he fell backwards into the water. The manager saw him and crashed through her back gate yelling, "What are you doing in that pool in the middle of the night with your *shoes* on!" Simon hauled himself out, took off his jeans and wrung them out saying, "Oh, hell, I *fell* in." And cypress trees . . .

I plead for the right to write. Type titles on envelopes for new poems and put dates of beginning and ending on each one and when the envelope's full file it in the big box, and yes and more and more until there is enough. I pretend that poetry readings are a joke:

Literary Criticism

If it's more work to read it
than it was to write it
burn it.

And continuing again, each time my life is broken into and, once more, beginning to continue. Always playing the Zen Buddhist whose work takes care of itself; I never admit that every line is an autopsy. I pray to the pictures on my desk: Sappho, Emily and Charlotte Bronte, Christina Rossetti and her mother, Virginia Woolf and *her* mother and so many more. Isadora Duncan and Gertrude Stein coming and going through my dreams and talking mostly about the sea. Gertrude noticed my house was ankle deep in sea water. She trudged 'round to the back where the breakers were knocking down the walls; the rust gave the thing the look of an ancient shipwreck. She seemed to enjoy wading in the tide pools, splashing and laughing.

In the serious mornings I take manuscripts to the post office and wait. An editor asks why I want to; I must remember to ask him the same. There is money to be had in the arts; Jim said so. There's money, he said, but don't depend on it, don't give it too much thought.

And the telephone: no, I can't come with you this time, I'm so afraid of dissipating the strength I haven't got . . . Rest: I'll get lots of rest now. Yesterday I went into a Rest Room. I imagined someone was dead in there in the little cabinet. I couldn't use the toilet because I was so sure someone in there was dead behind the door. And cypress trees . . .

And people: Sally can't go to Santa Cruz because her

brakes are sick but we can go to dinner and eat with chopsticks which is better than an evening with *him* because he is
so boring now and just wants fucking. I tell him it's like
sandwiches; there has to be something in between. He calls
it self-pity when I talk that way. I call it sadness. Kirsten says
she is always right in front of the fan when the shit hits.
Write poem: The Fan Dance. There was a woman lost her
wig in the wind today; lost her little reddish brown wig in
the wind on the street where it flew in among the cars like a
terrified puppy and the woman with her wisps of grey hair
ran here and there among the cars chasing her wig and the
high school girls snickered. And cypress trees . . .

Seven years until I'm fifty. Simon will be twenty-one.
Christina Rossetti was born on my birthday in 1830. She is
exactly 103 years older than I or I am exactly 103 years older
than she. Depending on how you look at it. Emily Dickinson
was born five days after Christina. I miss them.

There is still a great deal of work to be done. There are
lists to be made. For the long night cometh and the silence
and the cypress trees and the name of the star is called
wormwood. I wait for crib death among my middle-aged
friends. I say words and words, over and over, again and
again:

    laudanum — the wine of opium — laudanum
    septipara — a woman who has borne seven children —
    septipara
    thing — a Scandinavian assembly or court of justice
    during the middle ages — thing

What *do* people mean when they talk about things? Everyone is doing her/his own Scandinavian assembly. Yes. I must say words as long as I can. I must say everything until I can narrow things down and make them mean some thing, any thing, no thing.

I will write down the things as they happen; then I can follow the lines. Margaret came to stay. Just a nice quiet weekend, she said, no philosophy please. Passing me on the street a young black man stooped to look into my face. Was it so bad, Miss? he asked. I have read a story about Ruth Gordon and she says she might have married Alexander Woollcott except his glasses were always dirty. But these are events, not things. Things are what fall apart.

Last summer I found that oh-so-red starfish on the beach in Carmel and oh-so-red Simon said, it must have come from China, all the way. But I can't see so well this year and I fell in the sand and I lost it. I sat on the beach all evening beneath that twisted cypress tree at the bottom of the hill. I drank a whole bottle of wine: Big Sur Red. Poor old sea, I said, you're growing old.

winter 1977, Aptos, California

> "*How many black berries grow in the blue sea,
>   how many dark ships in the forest.*"
>   ballad

It's late in the 20th century and I'm walking to the end of the beach. Shall I write it all here, simply sitting down on the sand? Or should I walk to the end, to the place where I can't get through or over the rocks. Then, having seen it all from that direction, that is, going toward the end, should I turn around and write about it on the way back, reflecting on what is past? Is it all the same, coming and going? I won't remember it right. I forget the stagnant tide pool offshore when I'm walking next to the surf at the tide's edge where the pebbles crack and rattle like hailstones.

Maybe it's not possible to get to the *end*. It always starts again somewhere beyond. I've gotten as far as I am now. I tried to follow the shoreline as closely as possible, keeping one foot on the sand and one foot in the water. There is a place where the rocks can be penetrated but I always cut my feet and the beach on the other side of the stones looks very much like the one I'm on.

My friend Greta is sitting here under a cypress tree. She's bathed in the sun. She has made one trip up the hill to the Belladonna Bar. The old red lanterns are not lit. It's only afternoon. There is still a long evening to be lived. A nostalgia for nightshade is passing over me and my middle age shows. Greta says I'm a pain in the ass.

Greta and I have come to the sea to celebrate the annual

autumn mysteries; the Eleusian mysteries of Demeter and
Persephone. These are the old rites, the sea bathing, the
slaughter of pigs, purification, the final knowing and the
rebirth. For thousands of years before Christ, the Great
Goddess kept it together. I want to believe in the past and be
cleansed and go home to find Simon sitting with a new
Rapunzel. I want to know we're getting somewhere. I want
to laugh at them and call them the mermaid and the minotaur
and feel a part of living and cheer up. I know there is rebirth.
Time for a U-turn. Time to begin again beginning. If only I
could end this little book.

There is a voice in the passage. My left brain goes just so
far and then my right brain quits sending the messages.
There is a voice in the passage between my right brain and
my left brain and it screams *liar* and then it laughs.

They say when thought and feeling come together, the
words are true. All the feminists tell me so. So who is in the
passage laughing? They say that ancient wisdom is locked
inside us. All the psychics say so.

The word is revelation; the force that enables one thing
to create another. And words have failed me. Old words
were poems of connotations; they rang like bells. The awe is
gone. Now they, the words, are only kind or unkind. Is that
another lie? Greta wants a drink.

Greta's gone to the bar and I walk to the other side of the
hill. On the rocks by the water is a boy's tennis sock. An old
woman dusts the beach with a metal finder, looking for gold,
looking for anything she can find. I sit here with a bottle of
wine until the light is gone. I try to see my ancestors as they

crawled out of the sea. Birds flow past me, streaking through time. I fly too, I am flowing faster than ever before, but my mind says I am sitting here; I am so always here and always hearing seawolves howling and seeing the earth as a grave-yard of junked oceanic plates; a fatally fractured skull. (Hell, the best of Ireland is submerged. Old rock is always on top.)

I'll go find Greta. We'll get drunk. She'll say what she always says. Who needs another waste land. How's your sex life. I'll tell her how the world aches. She'll tell me I can't get away with it, it's only bad art.

Walking back to the cypress trees, I smoke a cigarette. It makes me stagger. Blonde, Germanic children are building a Byzantine sand castle. They pile auburn seaplants outside the moat to protect the sand. Sitting down, I try to write my thought and my feeling in the grains of sand. First I write in granulated sugar sand, baby soft and flour fine. Then I draw larger words in volcanic ash mixed with frail slivers of sea-shells. The colors are salmon, charcoal, toast, clorox-white and tell-tale grey. Every kind of sediment, stick, and stone is in the background. A living kelp crab crawls out from under a dead kangaroo crab. The stink of iodine and salt are so sharp, tears come to my eyes. I cannot make a picture on the sand. The Egyptians, I'll tell Greta, the ancient Egyptians didn't have a modern language so they couldn't argue about the meaning of words. Their words were signs, not symbols. That's why they lasted so long and stood so still. I make a circle in the sand around myself. I sit inside it.

Longing is all that lasts. The light goes quietly. After a while the sea grows dark. Down by the caves the great suicidal whale lies beached in the moonlight, crawling with creatures from the sand-strewn caverns of tonight. The townfolk cut away her head today. The rest will follow. She will burn. The marfire glows through the waves. Slowly the old woman comes. Demeter's mother walks by the sea. In the tide pools where the sea snakes hide, she gathers the salt weeds at ebb tide and brings the baskets home again.

About The Author

Jennifer Stone was born in December, 1933, in Tucson, Arizona. She has been based in Berkeley, California since 1951. She has two sons born in 1960 and 1962. Her last book, *Stone's Throw: Selected Essays*, published by North Atlantic Books in Berkeley, won the 1989 Before Columbus Foundation American Book Award. Her book on film and television, *Mind Over Media* was published in 1988 by Berkeley's Cayuse Press. Her first autobiographical fiction was a prose collection published in 1977 by the Berkeley Poets Workshop, *Over by the Caves*.

Her radio shows can be heard regularly on KPFA Pacifica Public Radio, 94 FM in Berkeley.